A TROPICAL HOLIDAY DUET

Elle Wright

Misty Urban

www.BOROUGHSPUBLISHINGGROUP.com

A TROPICAL HOLIDAY DUET
Copyright © 2023 Elle Wright and Misty Urban

ISBN 978-1-957295-64-0

EVERLASTING

A Letter Club Story

Elle Wright

CHAPTER ONE

Mayhem

Jonas

"Is it me, or was this easier twenty-five years ago?"

I grin at my wife, who's sitting kitty-corner at the breakfast table. "Ames," is all I say, knowing there's no need to respond to her rhetorical question.

She rolls her eyes and updates me on our winter holiday trip to Playa Negra in Costa Rica. We go back as often as we can to the place where we tied the knot. Not the marriage knot—that was three months after our first time at Playa Negra—but the knot that solidified what I'd known from the moment I'd first seen Amy in English Lit: she'd steal my heart, and I was more than fine with that since I never doubted we were meant to be together.

"Elaine was able to switch her flight so she'll arrive at Liberia Airport about forty-five minutes before we do. Then a shuttle is taking her to the private terminal to meet our plane." She's telling me something I already know about my mother flying in from L.A. But as a premier event planner, Ames can't help but recap out loud all the stuff she keeps in her head.

My Amy thinks in spreadsheets.

"Glad that worked out."

"Me too." She purses her lips in thought, and I can't help myself: I lean over the corner of the table and kiss her delicious lips. She puts her hands on my cheeks and kisses me back, sliding her tongue between my lips.

As I'm sifting my fingers through her hair, I hear, "Ugh. Really? Over breakfast?" Lei-lei, our ten-year-old, and our youngest, is free with her commentary, especially about her parents' displays of affection.

Amy and I smile as we separate and then look over at Lei-lei and Artie, who's twelve, and Lilli, who's fourteen, both of whom are standing next to the table behind Lei-lei.

"How'd you think they made four kids?" Artie says as he grabs a muffin out of the basket on the middle of the table, then plops down in a seat across from Amy.

"Like I wanna think about them"—Lei-lei throws out her arm in our direction—"doing it." She closes her eyes, shakes her head, and shudders.

"I think it's sweet," Lilli says as she sits next to Amy. Our Lilli loves her mom openly and adoringly.

"You think everything is sweet," Lei-lei jabs. "You're a walking, talking Pixy Stick."

Lilli, who is calm and composed almost all the time, never rises to the bait Lei-lei dangles in front of her sister's face all too often.

But Artie, who's a shit disturber, has no problem weighing in. "And you're a walking, talking Fizz Bomb."

"So not original." Lei-lei sits one seat away from Artie. "Who you cheat off to get those A's?"

Artie taps his temple and mutters with a mouth full of muffin, "Great brain."

"Debatable," Sam, our oldest at sixteen, says as he walks to the fridge, pulls out the egg tray, and holds it toward us. "I'm making a Swiss and spinach omelet. Who's in?"

Sam and Lilli got the cooking gene from me. Unfortunately, Artie and Lei-lei are like Amy. They can hardly boil water.

We all call out, "Me," and Sam starts making breakfast as Amy runs down the agenda for the next twenty-four hours.

"Everyone gets one rolly and a backpack. That's it. Pack smart, clean up your spaces, and that means under your bed. Your dad and I have some work to do, but we'll be in the house if you need us. There's enough food in the fridge for lunch. We're going out to dinner at Dive Bar Pizza. Everyone's butts in the SUV at six-thirty." Amy narrows her eyes. "Stragglers will be left behind."

Sam laughs, and Artie mutters, "Harsh."

"Tomorrow morning, we leave for JFK at five-thirty," Amy continues. Artie groans even louder than Lei-lei. "This is not news. Suck it up. The plane's coming in from Boston at eight-thirty, and we need to be buckled in by nine. The flight's five and a half hours, and their on-board media has all sorts of programs and movies. We talked about you bringing your personal devices. If you lose or break them, you pay to replace them, or go without, so choose wisely. Any questions?"

***

One good thing about waking our kids at 4:45 a.m. is they're asleep in the car on the way to the airport. Amy's dozing too. She stayed up way too late touching base with her staff to do final checks on all the events and parties her company's handling over the holiday season.

I can't help but smile thinking about how, when we got together, she was her company. A one-woman show. Now she has a staff of one hundred eighty people working in offices in New York, Chicago, L.A., and London. If she wanted, she could open an office in every major city in the world, but early on, she'd promised herself she'd keep her company manageable. She wanted to know each and every employee but made sure there'd be enough people to handle the work, but not so many that she didn't have a relationship with every one of them.

Her success exploded when she orchestrated the wedding of two wildly popular rock stars who wanted privacy. Amy managed to get one hundred of their closest friends and family to La Digue Island in the Seychelles. An island with no airport and less than three thousand residents. The friends and family had to take a ferry to La Digue, where they were the only guests at a sixty-three-villa luxury resort. The couple was married on Anse Source d'Argent beach, and the only photos taken were by the photographer Amy had hired who'd signed an ironclad non-disclosure agreement.

Three months after the rock stars were married, they released only one photo of the wedding, and the world media went wild. That's when Amy became as famous as her clients.

As I'm heading onto the access road to the private terminal at JFK, I turn on the radio loud enough to wake everyone gently. Various moans and groans turn into windows being lowered and shouts being hurled at Gio and Nat's kids as if they haven't seen them in years.

Nothing could be farther from the truth. Gio and Nat live in East Hampton, only fifteen minutes away from us, and are in our home as much as we're in theirs.

When Gio and I began working together on a medical and technical solution to detect and eliminate terminal diseases, Nat and Amy became fast friends. Both run their own companies, and both are wicked smart. Nat's something of a programming and hacking savant, and her innovations in system security have garnered her contracts with huge corporations and many governmental agencies.

I've barely pulled to a stop before the kids jump out of the car and head over to their friends. Sam and Bennie are the same age and have been tight since they were little boys. Isai is only a year older than Artie, and they've been buds since they were babies.

At eighteen, Dare, the oldest of Gio and Nat's kids, is close to Matt and Sofia's middle and youngest boys—his cousins—Luca and Rafe, nineteen and seventeen respectively.

Gio and I park our cars, and as we're heading to the terminal, Amy texts to tell us the plane has arrived from Boston. By the time Gio and I join the group, the din is so loud, we hang back and watch the show.

Gio's sister, Sofia, and her husband, Matt, are standing with Theresa—a psychologist who years ago literally stepped in front of a bullet meant for Sofia and saved her life—and her husband, Ethan, the intelligence analyst in charge of the Intelligence Division of the Boston FBI Field Office.

Which leads me to thinking about interesting and complicated relationships. Gio, Sofia, and Ro are the children of Alessandro Di Caro, a powerful and wealthy man many call Don Di Caro. Since saving Sofia's life, the don, who is one hundred percent old school, is indebted to Theresa forever. Which means he plays nice with her FBI husband.

I understand this better than most since my dad retired after a long career with the FBI. But he's made allowances for Don Di Caro because that man has been Amy's father in every way a man can and should be a father, and he's been there for her since she was seven years old.

Before he walked her down the aisle, he told her she was his third daughter, and since that day, and way before, he's stood by her as a good father would.

Because of all this history, Theresa and Ethan's children are part of what all the parents call "the pack." We started using that moniker when the kids were little.

Lia, Ethan and Theresa's oldest child, is twenty-four, goes to law school at NYU, and lives with Matt and Sofia's oldest, Alex, who's almost twenty-five and also goes to NYU's law school. Lia and Alex have been joined at the hip since they were babies.

Way back when, Amy told me they'd wind up together, and over the years I've learned never to doubt my wife's intuition.

Ethan and Theresa's son, Mikhail, who everyone calls Misha, is twenty-one and graduates from Yale in May. He plans to follow in his sister's footsteps but has been accepted to, and will attend, Yale Law School. Misha's closest friend in the pack is Alex, for obvious reasons.

Alex and Lia are running toward us along with Ro, Collin, and their twin thirteen-year-old girls, Olivia and Nicola. Nicola's named for Gio, Sofia, and Ro's *nonna*, who died seventeen years ago and was a great friend to Amy's grandmother, Lilli, for whom our daughter is named.

There are so many ways we're all connected, there's no denying we're family. Some by blood, all by love.

"We're not really late," Ro shouts as their group approaches. "We left the city at seven, got a great cabbie, but got stuck on the Triborough Bridge. Four-car pile-up. What a mess."

Collin—Ro's husband, Amy's childhood friend, and my college roommate—slings his arm around his wife's shoulders. "Do they look like they care?"

Ro stops and takes in the crowd. Most of us are grinning, smiling, or chuckling because Ro lives so out loud even when she doesn't have a reason, it makes all of us laugh. "Huh," she huffs. "I guess not."

Collin drops a kiss on her cheek, whispers something in her ear, and is rewarded with a bright smile from his wife.

As out loud as Ro is, that's how quiet, calm, and steady Collin is. Those two are all about balance.

Before we can do more than begin to exchange hugs with the New York City group, my wife and Sofia, best friends since the second grade, start walking toward the bathroom. Amy twirls her hand in the air, and then, as if choreographed, all the women and girls follow them to the bathroom, leaving us guys standing in a loose huddle looking a little stupid.

Ethan throws back his head and starts laughing, and through his laughter, he says, "Women. You gotta love 'em."

CHAPTER TWO

Mellow

Amy

I'm lying in a hammock strung to the roof of our bungalow's porch. What the resort calls a bungalow is really a large, round, freestanding hut with a thatch roof made from palm fronds with two hammocks hanging from the ceiling outside the front door, and a breakfast table and two chairs are on the side of the semicircular porch.

I'm lounging in one of my favorite outfits: a black-on-black paisley print tankini and a sarong with giant red hibiscus flowers against a black background, under which are black swim shorts. After four kids, my breasts are no longer in bikini shape, and my thighs don't know how to act if they're not encased in spandex.

Do I give a shit? Nope.

My Jonas still loves my body and can't wait to show me how much. And I do everything I can to show my appreciation by reciprocating in a variety of creative ways. As I had earlier this morning, using what he calls my *talented mouth*, to drive him crazy until he lost control. And when Jonas loses control…let's just say I'm sore in all the right places.

"I know what that smile means."

I open my eyes and grin at Sofia. "You're looking pretty loose your own self, *amica mia*."

"Damn straight." She uses her hand to fan her face. "Matt says the tropics makes him frisky."

"Good thing we're here for two weeks."

She puts her hand over her forehead. "I won't be able to walk after two weeks."

I'm laughing so hard I roll out of the hammock. "Don't make it sound like a complaint," I manage to spit out.

"I'm hoping the kids won't notice I'm walking funny."

"Soph. All the boys are together in that big two-story bungalow at the far end of the resort's property. Unless there's a medical emergency, or it's dinnertime, we won't see them until we leave for the airport."

"Doesn't that worry you?"

I shake my head. "Misha's twenty-one, Luca's nineteen, and Dare's eighteen. They'll keep an eye out for the two younger boys. So will Rafe, Sam, and Bennie. Rafe's seventeen, and Sam and Bennie are sixteen."

"Exactly. They're all walking testosterone factories." She points at herself. "Hello. I got knocked up at eighteen."

I smile huge. "To this day, I'll never forget the look on your father's face when Matt told him."

"I nearly shit a brick, Ames. Not a good memory."

"Ah, honey. But look how it turned out. Alex, Luca, and Rafe are the light in your dad's eyes. He knows your life's been filled with love, and although he won't say it, he knows Matt's a good man who adores you."

"Well, yeah. You're right about that."

I draw in a deep breath at the sight of what's approaching.

Sofia turns her head, then smiles at me. "It never gets old, does it?"

"Never," I whisper as I watch Jonas heading toward me, his surfboard under his arm, his body still dripping water, and his hair slicked back from his face. I've seen him like this at least a thousand times, but each and every time, my breath still catches and my heart skips beats.

He angles the board down and buries it into the sand before he comes to me, throws his arm around my shoulder, and lowers his head, inviting me to drink from his enticing lips. Never one to pass up a chance to taste him, I tilt my head up and enjoy a sweet, deep, all-too-short kiss.

Jonas smiles at Soph and asks, "Where's Matt?"

"When I left him, he was—"

"Recovering," I say.

"Relaxing in the hammock," Soph snaps.

I look up at Jonas and ask, "Don't you think it's cute she still blushes about having sex with Matt?"

He chuckles. "You're as big a troublemaker as Lei-lei."

As if conjured, Lei-lei's strawberry-blonde topknot bounces as she stomps over to us, Elaine following a few feet behind her. "I don't get—"

Jonas stares at our daughter and says, "Hello, Aunt Sofia. How are you?"

Lei-lei sighs so dramatically her shoulders go up and down. "Hello, Aunt Sofia. How's it going?"

Sofia's biting her lips to keep from laughing. "Hi, Lei-lei. It's going well. You?"

"Not so great." Lei-lei turns and, with her arm extended, points at Elaine. "I can't go anywhere or do anything without Mimi." Elaine refused to adopt any form of the word "grandparent" and settled on a popular alternative: Mimi.

"And your point is?" I ask.

"Lilli, Liv, and Nic are at the beach, hanging without supervision."

"Ah." Elaine wags her forefinger. "Luca, Sam, and Bennie are there with them."

"They're surfing," Lei-lei argues. "And you won't even let me do that. With them."

"No, we won't," Jonas states. "Big waves and experienced surfers is not a place for you to be surfing."

"Plus," I say, "one of them is always on the beach, keeping an eye on the girls while the others are surfing."

Lei-lei puts her hands on her hips. "Fine. Under protest, I'll stay with them on the beach."

Under protest. She's my kid, but I swear, sometimes I don't know where she comes from.

"Great," Elaine says. "I'll find someone to bring over a chair and an umbrella, and I'll hang at the beach too."

"I'm ten. Why don't you trust me?"

Jonas leans down. "It has less to do with your age and everything to do with your behavior."

Lei-lei glares at him. "That's not nice."

"Going into Sam's room and taking the box of condoms out of his nightstand and parading around the house with them wasn't nice," Jonas points out, and Sofia sucks in her lips.

"Pffft. It's not like everyone doesn't know he has them," Lei-lei defends.

"So you'd be okay with Artie going through your underwear drawer and taking out your psychedelic panties and parading them around the house?" I ask.

She scrunches up her nose, a female family trait I've passed down to our daughters.

"It's not like everyone doesn't know you wear underwear," Jonas says.

She lowers her head, but not in defeat. Oh no, not our Lei-lei. She'll marshal her defenses and live to fight another day.

"Okaaay. I'll go to the beach with Mimi."

Elaine claps. "Such a warm, pleasing pronouncement. I'm overwhelmed with love." Lei-lei turns and stomps away. Elaine says to us, "It's a damn shame weed isn't legal down here. Not lying, I need a whole bottle of edibles to endure the forty battles a day that girl generates."

We laugh, and Jonas says, "This is her version of mellow."

As she turns to follow Lei-lei, Elaine says, "I don't know where you get the strength."

I smile at Sofia and ask, "Still sorry you didn't have a girl?"

"At the moment, not so much."

***

Dinner is an event. There's twenty-five of us, and the restaurant has to push together tables to accommodate our group, which we split into two long tables. One for the adults, and one for the kids. Alex and Lia are definitely adults, but they don't want to sit and chat with their parents.

In what I consider a supreme sacrifice, they sit at the boys' end of the kids' table. Misha is close to them in age, so the three of them sort of huddle while the rest of the guys get to talk trash, and the girls have enough privacy at the other end of the table to whisper about all the things tweenies and young teenagers find fascinating.

Lei-lei hears all kinds of stuff she shouldn't hear at her age, which enhances her conviction she's one of them, which she most certainly is not.

The hotel staff are used to us. We've been coming here every other winter holiday break for fourteen years. Most of the staff have been here that long, and every visit, they comment on how many kids have been added to our families and at how much the kids have grown.

On the off years, each of us holiday with our parents. In our case, because we want to be somewhere warm, Jonas's dad, Skip, and his wife, Sharon, join us on our trip to Santa Monica. Elaine's house is too small for our brood, and while Elaine and Sharon get along well, no way are she and Skip staying with his ex.

Since we've been doing the family trek to California for a while, we have standing reservations at the Fairmont for a three-bedroom bungalow, and Skip and Sharon stay in a one-bedroom bungalow suite. Some days, Elaine comes over and hangs with us at the pool, and a lot of the time we all go up the PCH to Malibu to visit different beaches where Skip, Jonas, and the kids surf.

Gio, Sofia, and Ro's families go with their parents to Don Di Caro's private island in the U.S. Virgin Islands. Aside from the main house, the five-acre island has fourteen three-, four-, and five-bedroom villas, all with pools, which Don Di Caro built for his children and grandchildren.

For our twentieth wedding anniversary, the don gifted the island to us for a one-week stay. We ran naked on the beach and stayed naked as we went from villa to villa, behaving like we were still in college and not the parents of four children.

Ethan and Theresa make the rounds. Ethan's parents live in a tiny town in central Oregon, and his brother and his family, who live in Portland, join them for the holidays. Theresa has family in Northern California, and her father accompanies them when they go west to visit. Her mother died eight years ago, and Ethan and Theresa visit her dad, and her sister and her family, in Connecticut frequently.

To say we're all busy is an understatement. But we find time and a way to be together as often as possible. Jonas promised me life-long love and family, and he delivered in spades.

I'm staring at the kids' table, watching how animated and close our children are with one another, when I feel Jonas squeeze my knee.

"What's up?" he whispers.

I smile and put my hand over his heart. "I'm soaking it in. It's so fabulous, sometimes I can hardly believe it's real."

"My Amy." He hugs me against his side and keeps his arm draped over my shoulder.

He didn't need to say more than those two words.

In them I heard all the love we've shared, and all the love we will share.

CHAPTER THREE

Colpo di fulmine

Bennie

Fuck. Shit. Dammit.

I shouldn't be doing this. I know I shouldn't be doing this, but it seems to be out of my control. I'm a Di Caro, and I've heard all the stories. We've all heard all the stories about how my *nonno* couldn't imagine living his life without our *nonna*, so he proposed on their second date. How my father fell in love with my mother through anonymous letters. How my Aunt Sofia fell in love with Uncle Matt when she was seventeen, and then he knocked her up when she was eighteen. How my Aunt Ro made stealth incursions until Uncle Collin didn't ask or say a word before he moved in with her and never left.

Then there's my great Aunt Toni, my *nonno*'s youngest sister by thirteen years who married great Uncle Aaron, a Jewish guy who grew up on a kibbutz. He was in law school, and she was halfway through her freshman year when they met. He knocked her up when she was a junior, and they went to Maryland and got married by a hippie rabbi. Toni and Aaron have eight kids, who they raised Jewish, and they still live in their farmhouse in upstate New York, where they grow all their own organic fruits and veggies.

So, the lore of *when we know, we know* isn't bullshit. It's in our blood, and, apparently, there's no escaping it.

I'm sixteen years old, and I know shit. Yeah, I get good grades, I'm a bit of a history buff, and I stay up on current events, but I'm a long fucking way from being old enough to decide who I'm going to spend the rest of my life with. Yet, unfuckinbelievably, I know.

Freakishly, knowing isn't the problem. I mean, yeah, it's a weight that hit me like a meteor landing on my head, but it's her, and it'll always be her. And I'm good with that.

Who she is? Well, that's a swamp filled with alligators, vipers, and flesh-eating bacteria. Everyone I love is going to hate me, and my best friend is going to tear my dick from my body with one hand.

It all started totally innocently. Truly. We grew up together.

My father's a medical doctor, and Uncle Jonas has a PhD in medical robotics. They became besties, research associates, and business partners. They have a company, in partnership with doctors and PhDs in Australia, called Detecto-Bots, which makes swarm-bots that go into a diseased person's body, find the disease, send back info, and then nanobots go through the body and kill the disease at a cellular level.

Totally true and amazingly cool, my dad, Uncle Jonas, and their Australian partners found a way to eradicate cancerous cells in people's bodies.

Because Uncle Jonas and Dad are friends and business partners, we live fifteen minutes away from them, and the company is only a half hour away from Uncle Jonas's house.

We're in each other's homes all the time, and our families do almost everything together. We're so intertwined, it's ridiculous. Aside from the intensely close relationship Aunt Amy has with my mom, Aunt Amy has been best friends with Aunt Sofia since they were in second grade, and she practically grew up in my *nonno* and *nonna*'s house.

In other words, everyone is going to want to kill me.

Even when we were little, the boys played with the boys, and the girls played with the girls. Five boys and two girls, both sisters who are Uncle Jonas and Aunt Amy's kids.

Lilli and Helen, who everyone calls Lei-lei.

Lilli's always been calm and quiet, a direct contrast to Lei-lei, who could level buildings with her little-girl glare.

Lilli's always been more girly than Lei-lei, who could play rugby for the New Zealand All Blacks.

Lilli has dark blonde hair that lightens in the summer, and it's so pretty when the light blonde and dark blonde mix and layer, especially when she wears her hair up in a messy knot on the top of her head.

Recently, she stopped cutting her hair, which used to skim her shoulders, and now it's grown halfway down her back.

Even when she was little, she was always a looker. She's the female version of her father, who, years ago, modeled to help pay for college. Actually, he was famous, and every so often my dad teases him by calling him "pretty boy."

Since she's two years younger than me, we'd talk at the dinner table, or when we were at the beach, or lying by the pool, and most of it was the kind of things guys say to younger female family members.

But something changed.

Actually, a lot of somethings changed, and all of a sudden, Sam's sister became way more than an extended part of my family: she became a person unto herself.

And I became intrigued.

Her long hair bounces against her back when she walks, and she's not walking like a kid anymore, she's walking like a teenage girl. Not really swaying her hips as much as her hips sway because she's a little curvy now.

When she smiles, which she does a lot, it's cute and kind of shy.

She's taken to polishing her fingernails and toenails the same color. Today I saw they were hot pink.

She doesn't wear make-up, but her lips are always shiny, so I'm guessing she puts on lip gloss.

And yesterday, the first day we were at the beach, when she pulled off her long beach shirt, she wasn't wearing a one-piece Speedo—she was wearing a two-piece with a ruffly top in black and white that she filled out nicely, and black bottoms that looked like sexy underwear cut way higher on her hips than a Speedo.

At the sight of her, two thoughts went through my head simultaneously: she looks sweet and sexy cute, and I'll kill any guy who lays a hand on her.

On this family vacation, part of all the guys' jobs is when we're surfing, hanging out on the beach, or are by the bungalows, we have to keep an eye on the girls. Which isn't a hardship since they're funny and easy to be around.

But even though Lilli's only a year older than Liv and Nic, she doesn't look like she belongs with them anymore. The twins look like kids. Lilli looks like dessert.

But, fuck. She's only fourteen, and no matter that I'm only two years older than her, those two years might as well be fifteen. She's too fresh, and I'm too experienced. I'm not a fuck-boy, though her brother is, and that's not something I'll tell anyone, but I've had my fair share of pussy.

Both Sam and I are on the youngest end of the cutoff for when we started school, so we're two of the youngest juniors in high school, and when we graduate we'll be seventeen and a half.

But age doesn't factor in that much in high school. Looks, sports, and grade level matter.

I have my parents to thank for my good genes both in looks and physicality. I'm captain and goalie of the soccer team, and I'm six-one. Girls go for that kind of shit. But none of the ones I've fucked care that I have a 3.95 GPA, or that I speak Italian fluently. I'm as much a peg on their board as they're a notch on my belt. Mutual gratification with no strings attached.

Lilli's not going to be anyone's notch. No one but me is ever going to touch her. And I'm going to have to wait at least two years before I'll be able to cop a feel, never mind how long it's going to take before I'm balls deep inside her.

And because I'm a Di Caro, and in my blood I'm programmed to be a one-woman man, I'm gonna have a wicked right hand by the time I make Lilli mine.

Shit. My balls hurt just thinking about it.

So now I've had two days of Lilli in a sweet two-piece. Today she wore a super light-green long-sleeve crop top with a pretty skimpy bikini bottom in the same color. She was way more covered than almost all the teenage girls on the beach, but seeing her sweet curves and her long, long legs on display, I made sure I sat damn close to her when it was my turn to hang out with the girls.

Without acting like I was interested, but I'm completely interested in everything Lilli is doing and saying, I'd noticed she was reading an actual book, and asked, "Paperback, huh?"

"I've got a thing for the way books smell," Lilli said. I raised my brow. "Do you ever go to the library?"

"Yeah. At school, all the time."

"Doesn't it smell great?"

I grinned. "Actually, no. It smells a little better than the locker room, but not by much."

She scrunched up her nose, and damn if that wasn't adorable. "Ew."

"Yeah, ew." I wasn't going to tell her teenage boys stink from hormones oozing out of every pore on their body. The stench in the library is especially strong since the heat is always on too high, which makes us stink even more than we usually stink.

"How about the East Hampton library? Ever been there?" she asked.

"Mom used to take us when we were little. They had kids' events and stuff like that."

"You should go in and take a deep breath. No ew. I promise."

Yeah, even from that one conversation, I could see how I'd be in deep with her for the rest of my life. She's sweet. Not sugary. More like considerate and gentle. Something to look forward to coming home to every night.

I'm walking back to the big bungalow that sleeps eight, which means each of us has our own room, and I couldn't be more grateful for having the ability to have a good night's sleep for the entire vacation.

Sam, who's usually my roommate, doesn't snore, but he's a restless sleeper who sometimes sounds like he's fighting a battle with the sheets. Artie farts all night, Rafe and Luca snore like they're sawing wood, and Dare, Misha, and Isai talk in their sleep.

According to Sam, I snore lightly when I first fall asleep, but for the rest of the night I'm out cold. I've never slept with any of the girls I've fucked, so I've gotta take Sam's word as truth.

"Yo, hold up," Sam calls. I stop and wait for him. He stands his surfboard in the sand and says, "Watch this, will ya? Mimi texted. She left her hat on the beach. I'm going back to get it, then we'll stop by the girls' bungalow to drop it off."

I nod, and he jogs off.

If Lilli's walking around in that two-piece, I'm going to have to make sure I keep my expression neutral and my gaze on anyone or anything else. Otherwise, Sam's bound to pick up on where my attention's focused, and I have no intention of getting into it with him.

I plan on keeping my shit together for as long as possible, and if I don't fuck up, I won't have to get into it with him for at least another couple of years.

CHAPTER FOUR

Wildest Dreams

Lilli

Hoo-boy and holy shit. Two mornings in a row of all my dreams coming true. Since I was six and Bennie was eight, I've been madly in love with him. I bet he doesn't even remember this, but the memory is seared into my brain and is why, even at six, I knew he's my *one*: We were at his grandparents' house in Connecticut for some party, and I was going outside to sit by the pool when their little dog, Piccolo, ran out before I could close the door. He took off like a shot and headed toward the woods at the back of the property. I didn't want him to get hurt, so I ran after him and got lost. Bennie found me and held my hand the whole way back to the house while telling me how brave I was for trying to catch Piccolo, who, it turned out, was fine and already back in the house.

Even as a young boy, Bennie was gorgeous. Tall with thick dark brown hair and light brown eyes, he was always smiling. Always happy. I saw him a lot because he and my brother, Sam, have been best friends since they were infants. Their birthdays are three weeks apart, and since our parents are super close, Sam and Bennie even shared a crib when they were babies.

I remember him always being nice to me. He didn't tell me to get away when I tried to play with him, his older brother, Dare, and

Sam. Bennie called me Goldilocks and said the boys were the three bears.

As it would, things changed when we were in school where being two years older than me meant we hardly saw each other. Different floors, different lunch times, and after school, he and Sam went to soccer practice. Most weekends there were soccer matches or baseball games, and I saw Bennie, but we didn't spend much time together.

When he went to middle school, I never saw him unless he was at our house after practice or at a game. In the summers, our families spent a lot of time at the beach, and when we were old enough, we went to surf day camp for a couple of weeks and horseback riding day camp for another couple of weeks.

I still ride, but not competitively. When I'm older and I'm earning my own money, I'm going to buy a place where I can have stables. I love horses and dogs. Dogs, rescue dogs, have always been a part of our family. Right now, we have two mutts. One, Ella, is part Lab for sure. She loves the water and is always in the pool, and she goes nuts when we bring her to the beach. The other, Bruiser, is mostly a Boxer, and he chases everything that moves. Even the crickets aren't safe from him.

I surf, but not like my brothers and the Di Caro boys. They attack the waves like they're at war with the water. I can't keep up with them and I don't even try. I like to surf with my dad, who's laidback and easygoing. Even though he lived there for only a few years, he still has a lot of SoCal vibes.

When I went to middle school, Bennie was in eighth grade. I saw him only once in a while in the halls, and he was never alone. He always had a girl with him. Frequently, two or three. I was a sixth grader, and he was already one foot out the door, heading for high school.

Even though I didn't like seeing those girls hanging all over him, I wasn't worried. Somewhere deep inside me, I knew he was mine, and when the time was right, he'd know I was his.

This year, when I became a high school freshman, I began to doubt my convictions. Almost every girl in school, from freshman to senior, has tried to become my new best friend. Apparently, Sam and Bennie are prime meat, and everyone wants a bite.

I've been invited to tons of parties I wasn't allowed to go to, and I always have a least twenty girls sitting around me at the soccer games, all of them panting for Sam or Bennie to smile or wave at me. Which, duh, never happens.

One time, Sam was yellow-carded, and he texted me to go to his car and get his jacket. It was chilly, and he expected to be benched the rest of the game. I hold on to his keys since he's always losing them, so I texted back "Okay" and went down the bleachers to head to his car.

No lie, I had ten girls walk with me to his car—they oohed and aahed over a ten-year-old Camaro—then followed me back to the field, where I shouted, "Sam," three times before he turned around and ran over to grab his jacket and mumble, "Thanks."

On the way back to the bleachers, those girls said the stupidest things: "He has such a deep voice." "Did you see his thighs?" "And that wavy auburn hair?" "What about those green eyes? Yum."

I wanted to tell them to "shut up," but they probably wouldn't've heard me as they kept picking over him like carrion on a carcass.

Sam's my big brother and can be a pain in the ass. Not as big a pain as Artie, but Sam has his moments. Yet, I can be objective and state: Sam's really good-looking. He got Dad's surfer dude body type and Dad's moss-green eyes, but Sam inherited Mom's auburn hair right down to the waves.

Artie and I have Dad's dark blond hair, which lightens in the summer. That means I've got streaks I don't have to pay for. Artie, Lei-lei, and I all have Mom's golden-brown eyes, and Lei-lei's strawberry-blonde hair is what Mimi calls a red-blonde combo smashup.

With all the attention Bennie gets, and all the gossip I hear since packs of girls sit around me at lunch, I can't help but hear every scrutinized moment of Bennie's life.

My first semester in high school sucked pretty large.

But all my tomorrows changed yesterday morning, and all my doubts and worries were carried away by a warm tropical breeze.

The guys had been tasked with keeping an eye on us, even though Mimi is never more than twenty feet away. They rotate surfing, with one of them coming to sit with us girls until someone else takes over. When it was Bennie's turn, I caught him doing a head-to-toe body sweep, and his expression went from friendly to really, really, *really* friendly.

Butterflies started beating their wings inside my stomach, and my breath seemed to've left my body. He smiled like he knew I was all discombobulated, but he made small talk about me working after school twice a week at the stables so I can ride for free on the weekends. And I swear, it was like he was trying to calm me.

Then this morning, when it was his turn to sit with us, he didn't even pretend he wasn't interested in me and what I was doing. Right away, he picked up my book, and we started talking about reading and libraries.

The good thing about knowing Bennie all my life is I've seen with my own eyes that he's a good guy. I don't have to go through the getting-to-know-you stage, and I don't have to worry I'm hearing exaggerations or lies. I'm certain I don't know everything about him, but I'm guessing I'd have a ninety percent accuracy rate when it comes to Beniamino Dante Di Caro.

Lei-lei and Mimi had just come back from a walk along the shoreline, and I saw storm clouds circling Lei-lei's head. As she stomped off, Mimi called out to Bennie, "Stay with the girls," then followed Lei-lei between the tall palm trees and headed toward the bungalows.

Nic smiled at Bennie and said, "Looks like you're stuck with us."

He shook his head. "Nah, I'm good. You have cards with you?" Liv produced a deck out of her little backpack. "Great. Gather up some sea shells and we'll play poker."

"Let's play for money," Nic said.

"Seashells, *la mia piccola giocatrice d'azzardo*."

"What does that mean?" Nic snapped.

"My little gambler." Bennie shook his head. "I have to have a word with my aunt if you don't know enough Italian to understand me."

"I know all the curse words. She uses them a lot."

He laughed, then said, "I bet."

Our family plays cards, especially in the winter when the weather keeps us inside. My mom learned from her grandma Lilli, for whom I'm named. We sit on opposite sides of the dining room table, boys versus girls, and overall, we girls win sixty-seven percent of the time. Mom keeps track. She's super organized, and her whole life, business and personal, is filled with spreadsheets.

Mostly, we play gin rummy, but Sam and Mom love poker, so I've gotten pretty good at it. We play for chores. Whichever team loses, they have to do the other team's chores for the next day. It doesn't sound like much, but when we play for a couple of hours, the chores pile up, and the losing team could get stuck with one month's worth of the winning team's chores.

Except for cooking. Only me, Sam, and Dad are "allowed" to cook. When it's Mom's turn to assume Dad's chores, he helps her when it comes to cooking. Actually, they help each other with everything.

But when it comes to cooking, he makes her his sous chef, so she chops up stuff and things like that. He does the actual cooking because she's terrible at it. Same goes for me and Sam. We can cook, but Artie and Lei-lei are only allowed to do prep help. They're even worse than Mom. Though, I gotta say, Artie tries. Lei-lei avoids all chores any time she thinks she can get away with it.

So, there we were on a white sand beach, sitting on a giant blanket under a giant umbrella, while the fronds on the palm trees separating the beach from the bungalows and buildings were making a scratching noise as the breeze picked up. It was late morning and about eighty-five degrees. A total slice of paradise.

After he dealt, Bennie put a large sea shell on the card deck to keep them from blowing away. Liv, who's clueless when it comes to cards, was Bennie's partner. Nic and I were partners. Nic's ruthless, and I'm skilled. I figured we were going to kick their asses.

The first time Bennie caught me stealing a glance at him, I dipped my head and looked down at my cards, hoping I wasn't doing anything stupid like blushing. Or drooling.

A few hands later, he was watching me, and he didn't look away. It felt like he wanted me to know I had his full attention.

I don't know how to flirt, but after he held my gaze and smiled, I didn't look away anymore.

Bennie, who's played cards at our house, is really good at it. So, although Liv was horrible, Bennie managed to hold up their end. We won more hands than they did, but we weren't kicking their asses.

At the same time Luca came over to sit with us, Mimi and Lei-lei returned to the beach, Lei-lei looking more unhappy than when she'd left. Love my sister, I really do, but she's a handful and has been since before she was born. When Lei-lei gets on Mom's last nerve, Mom reminds her that she's the only one of her children who gave her morning sickness.

Luca stayed with us until Bennie and Sam came out of the water, and then we headed back to our bungalows.

The guys never eat lunch with us. They have a kitchen in their huge bungalow and prefer hanging there. My guess, they don't change out of their wet board shorts, eat tons of junk food, talk trash, and are disgusting. Artie and Isai have burping and farting contests all the time, and the other guys bet on who's gonna win. They can't do any of that in the restaurant.

Since my crop top is dry, and the restaurant where we eat lunch is casz, I put on a pretty sarong with yellow and green tropical birds over my bathing suit bottom.

I'm walking onto the porch and nearly bump into Sam. Bennie's standing a few feet away from the bungalow next to his and Sam's surfboards, which are planted in the sand. Bennie glances at me, grins, then drops his head to look at his feet.

"What's up?" I ask.

Sam pushes a hat into my hand. "Give this to Mimi. She left it on the beach." He turns and jogs down the steps.

I don't think, I just blurt out, "Why don't you guys have lunch with us?"

"Nah, sis. We've got things on." As Sam yanks his surfboard out of the sand, Bennie looks up and smiles.

As he's walking away with his surfboard under his arm, he turns his head and winks.

CHAPTER FIVE

Still the One

Natalia

One of the things about having a partner who knows you down to the ground is how their facial cues can tell a story, and no one who's watching knows what the hell we're saying to each other.

Last night, after the kids went back to their bungalows, leaving the ten parents to a night cap, I felt Gio staring at me. I turned and saw his half-smirk and thought: Game on.

We waited about ten minutes before standing and saying our goodnights before heading to our bungalow. He'd barely closed the door when I dropped to my knees, unzipped his jeans, yanked them down his fantastic thighs, and sucked his beautiful cock into my mouth.

We've been together for twenty-five years, and we still act like horny teenagers.

And we're not quiet about it.

Which is why, when we found the house we've called home for twenty-one years, Gio told the contractor who was updating the kitchen and bathrooms, to soundproof our bedroom.

There've been plenty of days when I hardly had the energy to drag myself downstairs for a cup of coffee, but no matter how busy we are, and how exhausted we feel, we've always had time and energy for each other.

Gio is a rare person. Strong, smart, driven, passionate, considerate, and devoted. He's my best friend, and my warrior renaissance man. It doesn't hurt that he's extraordinarily handsome and is sexy as fuck, but that's an external boon. In everything that matters, he's my gift who keeps on giving.

Which is why, after fucking our brains out until four in the morning, I let him sleep, knowing that telling him what I have to tell him can keep until much later this morning.

***

We're having a quiet late breakfast on the porch of our bungalow. Gio eats light in the morning, and I eat like I'm going into battle, which, given my business, isn't an exaggeration. He has fruit and yoghurt sprinkled with granola, and I'm eating a frittata with a side of hashbrowns.

"All right, Ace. Spit it out."

Yep, knows me down to the ground. Even if I wanted to, which I don't, I could never hide anything from him.

"Dare applied to the Air Force Academy. His backup school is Brown."

"That's it? What happened to 'four Ivies, and I'll probably go to law school?'"

I shake my head. "I don't know. You heard the same thing I heard back in September. I didn't see the need to chase him about his applications because it's Dare. His grades are great, he has a ton of extracurriculars, and he's responsible. He's a double legacy at Brown, and nobody in the northeast doesn't know the Di Caro name"—I rub my middle finger and thumb together—"so there isn't an Ivy that wouldn't take him."

Gio's expression is riding incredulous and is halfway between *what the fuck* and *why wouldn't my boy talk to me.* "Did he tell you?" he asks. I shake my head. "How'd you find out?"

"Francesca."

"My mother knew?"

"This is what she said to me: In mid-November, Dare went to his grandfather and told him about the Air Force application and how he needed some weighty recommendations. Your father was as perplexed as we are and questioned Dare, who told him he'd thought long and hard about how best to help society and decided to serve his country by being a fighter pilot."

Gio rubs between his eyebrows with his two middle fingers. "This doesn't make sense. He's never been a fighter, and he's never been into planes. Where the hell is this coming from?"

"I don't know. Your father tried to suss out the root of his decision, and you know if anyone can get answers from someone, it's your dad. But Dare stuck to his story, and your father agreed to help him and got a congressman and a state senator to write recommendations. Apparently, Dare's met both of them as they'd been at a couple of meet-your-representatives things the high school puts together for the seniors to coincide with them registering to vote.

"And, although she didn't say so, I'm guessing your father's troubled by Dare's decision and spoke to your mother about it, knowing she'd tell me and I'd tell you."

"My old man." He closes his eyes. "Why didn't he call me before he asked those politicians for favors?"

I shrug. "There's precious little your father does that I understand or can explain."

"That makes two of us." Gio sighs. "So what now?"

"There are two approaches, and I'm not sure which is best. We can take the low-stress approach and talk to him here where it's quiet and relaxing, or let him enjoy his vacation and talk to him when we get home."

"You can sit on this for a couple of weeks?"

"Not my first choice, but we need to be strategic. Where would he be most likely to tell us what the fuck is really going on?"

Gio turns his head and looks toward the beach. We can't see the water from here, but we can hear the ocean as if it's only feet away. Between us and the sea, there are too many palm trees for a view, and, intentionally, because we're noisy, we took the bungalow farthest away from everyone.

It doesn't matter where we're sitting. Being here, looking at the palm trees and listening to the tropical birds' squawks and calls are as soothing as the lapping ocean. While hanging here on the porch, I've seen a toucan, a scarlet macaw, and a great green macaw.

I reach across the table and squeeze his hand. "What do you think we should do?"

"Honestly, I'm going have *agita* unless we talk to him now. We've always been *put your cards on the table* parents. Why change now?"

"Okay. How about we ask him to have lunch with us on the beach?"

"You can eat after that breakfast?"

I widen my eyes. "Like you don't know I can eat all day long."

"Where do you put it, Ace?"

"Sex fuel."

He grins. "Knock yourself out."

"Pshaw. That's your job."

He tilts his head back and laughs, and I think: My work here is done.

***

We ask the staff to set up a table and umbrella at the far end of the beach, away from the restaurants and most of the bungalows. It's not private, but it's quiet, and at this hour, and on this end, the beach is relatively empty. We'll have to wait longer for our food, but we're so worried about Dare, it doesn't matter.

I can't help running a mental slideshow of Dare as a baby, a toddler, his first day of kindergarten, his first big-boy tooth, the first time he scored a goal for his soccer team, and every first I can remember, and I remember them all.

Now, as I see him walking down the beach, I see nothing of me. Externally, he's one hundred percent his father. Tall, broad shoulders, long legs, dark hair, and bright blue eyes. He has his father's straight nose, full lips, and magnificent cheekbones. Yet, his personality is seventy-five percent me. The twenty-five percent that's Di Caro is the over-protective, hot-headed, *I'll take care of everything…* And that's when it hits me. Dare's doing this for a girl.

But who? As far as we know, he plays the field. Not as much as Bennie, but Dare dates, though no one lasts more than a month.

Before Dare gets too close to hear, I lean over the table and say, "Hold on to your shorts, babe. I just figured out…this is about a girl."

Gio hides his surprise as he stands and hugs Dare, who turns and hugs me.

A waiter comes over to the table and takes our drink orders. I want a clear head, and I'm sure Gio feels the same way. We all order the house lemonade that's made with a dash of mango purée.

"I'm guessing you spoke with *Nonno*?" Dare says.

Yep, our kid is smart and, like me, cuts right to the heart of the matter.

"Actually," I say, "your grandmother was functioning as your grandfather's conduit."

He gives me a grin so like his father's it's uncanny. "That sounds about right."

Gio chuckles, then, following his son's cue, cuts to the heart of the matter. "Your mom thinks you're doing what you're doing for a girl."

Dare's brows go up, his eyes widen, and his lips part. "Is that a Romani thing? You know, like a seer. I've heard there's a lot of Roma in Ukraine. Maybe you're Roma."

Gio shakes his head. "It doesn't matter how she knows, only that she knows."

Dare mimics his father's head shake. "Okay. Yeah. It's about a girl."

"We're going to need more than that." Gio rolls his finger in the air.

Dare takes a deep breath, and I can tell he's been struggling with this for a while. "So, Hannah Baranski was a counselor at the same day camp I worked at last summer. I knew her from school, but we never really talked or anything. Different crowd." He sighs. "Anyway, we started hanging out, and, well, I, ah, really liked her, so we hung out a lot."

Gio and I hold each other's gazes for a moment in mutual understanding that "hanging out a lot" means they're having sex.

"When we went back to school, we kept seeing each other."

"Is there a reason you didn't bring her home to meet us?" I ask.

"Yeah."

Gio does the finger roll again.

"Her parents are pretty strict and don't want her dating non-Jewish guys."

Gio asks, "You tell Hannah we've got a lot of Jewish family members?"

"Yeah, but since I'm not one of them, I'm off limits."

"Which doesn't explain why we didn't meet her." Gio's getting annoyed.

"She's embarrassed about her parents and didn't want to make you guys feel"—Dare shrugs—"I don't know, awkward."

"I can understand that." I've gotta cool this down before Gio blows a gasket. "She's sensitive to other people's feelings. That's a good quality to have."

Dare nods. "Yeah, she is sensitive." He looks at Gio. "Then things went crazy in her house. Her brother moved to Israel after high school and joined the Israeli army. In late September, during the shelling, he was hurt."

"Oh, no." No doubt her parents went crazy. I'm going crazy thinking about my boy joining the Air Force.

"He's okay now. They pulled some shrapnel out of his leg, and he's back on active duty. But Hannah's folks have gone off the deep end, and they're making her feel all kinds of guilty for being with me, and for living this cush life in the U.S. They're making all kinds of noise about moving to Israel permanently."

He drags his fingers through his hair, just like Gio. "Next thing I know, she's applied to the Air Force Academy so she can prove to her parents she's like her brother, and since everyone knows the U.S. supports Israel's military, she figures this is as good as being over there." Dare shakes his head. "It's fuckin' nuts. I've tried to talk her out of it, but it's like she's gone deaf to reason."

Gio closes his eyes, which I know is one of his ways to mine for patience. After a long moment, he looks at Dare and says, "So you figured you'd go to the Academy to keep her safe."

Dare nods.

Shit. He's exactly like his father. "You love her."

Dare gives me a lopsided smile. Exactly like his father's. "Yeah."

Well, that's that. Once a Di Caro falls, they're all in. I know this to be an absolute truth as I've been living it for twenty-five years, plus I've seen it happen repeatedly throughout the family.

"Since we don't want you to do something that's noble but not what you want for yourself, what can we do to help keep Hannah from going to the Academy for all the wrong reasons?" Gio asks.

My man. Such a good guy.

"I swear, Dad. If I knew the answer to that, I'd've done it myself."

"Well, now that we know what we're facing"—Gio leans forward and wraps his hand around the back of Dare's neck—"we have time to put our heads together to find a solution."

"Right," Dare says as he grabs onto Gio's wrist.

"Does Bennie know?" I ask.

"Yeah." Dare smirks at me, and Gio releases his hold. "Don't tell him I told you this, but he keeps saying I should bring Hannah home so you can straighten her out."

Gio smiles. "Another smart son. And a good idea."

"Don't make it a thing," I tell him. "Bring her over on a Sunday afternoon, and we'll play cards, eat junk food, and talk shit."

Dare grins. "You're going to loosen her up before you put the whammy on her."

I'm laughing. "Put the whammy on her?"

"Yeah, Mom. You do it to us all the time." I raise one brow. "Okay, like the time Bennie dented his front fender, but it was below the deductible, so it was an out-of-pocket expense. You told him to get an estimate, and he thought you meant you guys were going to pay for it. When he brought you the estimate, and you told him you'd work it out tomorrow, he was sure he was off the hook.

"Then the next day, after you must've called around to find the prices of the services you were going to inflict on Ben, you gave him all these jobs to do around the house. Like painting the interior of the garage, which required him to clean out the garage. Once he did all the work that equaled the cost of the car repair, you gave him the money to get the dent fixed." Dare sat back and brushed his hands together in an *all done* move. "You put the whammy on him."

***

"Ace." Gio's wearing one of my favorite expressions. Spent, and completely satisfied.

"Hmm?" I lower my head and hum into the side of his chest as I throw my arm across his still-rock-hard abs.

"Baby, you put the whammy on me."

I lift my head and smile wide. "I did that twenty-five years ago. Since then, I've been administering daily maintenance injections."

He pulls on a hank of my hair and starts playing with it. "Lucky me."

"Lucky us." I feel myself beginning to drift to sleep, but before I do, I need to say, "You know we're going to be meeting our future daughter-in-law soon."

He lays his hand on my ass and squeezes. "Yeah. Big changes coming. It's a lot." He sighs. "We weren't that young."

"A couple, three years older. We had some life under our belts, but not much."

"When you know—"

"You know."

"Love you, Ace."

"Lucky me."

"Lucky us."

CHAPTER SIX

Landslide

Bennie

"Was it brutal?" I ask Dare, who's sitting on the edge of my bed.

"Nah. You know how they are. United front and totally cool. Mom figured out a way to bring Hannah over to the house so Mom can lay the whammy on her and get her to see how going into the Academy makes no sense."

"Did Mom say 'the whammy?'"

"No, you idiot. She didn't even know what the whammy was until I explained it to her. She thought it was funny."

"Brother, there is *nothing* funny about Mom's whammies."

"There is, as long as she's not laying them on you."

He's not wrong. I sigh, knowing I have to talk to Dare about Lilli. If I don't get this shit off my chest, I'm afraid I'm going to explode. Or is it implode? Whatever. I'm losing my fuckin' mind.

Dare's brows pinch together and drop just like Dad's do. "What? You look like you're in pain."

"I am." He pulls his phone out of his back pocket. "What are you doing?"

"Calling Dad."

"Why?"

"You said you're in pain."

I smack the phone out of his hand. "Asshole. Not that kind of pain." Dare glares. "Okay. It's sort of physical, but it's because of what I'm dealing with."

Dare climbs all the way on the bed, stuffs a pillow behind his back, and posts up against the headboard. "What are you dealing with?"

"Why do I feel like you've become a shrink?"

"Why do you feel like I've become a shrink?"

I punch the bed beside his hip. "Stop fucking around and pay fuckin' attention."

He grins. "You know, you say fuck in almost every other sentence."

I grit my teeth. "I'm going to fuck you up. How's that for proper usage?"

He bugs out his eyes, but he must see the smoke coming out of my ears, so he says, "All right. What's going on?"

"First, you have to promise to listen all the way through without saying or doing anything."

"Like doing what?"

"I really need you to promise."

"Ah, I think we've just moved into *oh fuck* territory," he mutters.

"Sort of. It has *oh fuck* potential, but I'm doing everything I can to not take it there." He stares, and I shake my head. "You know how we are?" He raises those thick brows. "I mean the Di Caros. When it comes to falling for someone. Like how you fell for Hannah and are ready to go to the Air Force Academy to keep her safe. You *know* how we are."

"Right. Yeah. I know."

"Well. I'm fucked. I really, really wish this happened like four or five years from now. Six or seven would be even better. But, no shit, it hit me like a category five hurricane, and I'm all in. Sunk. That's it. She's it for me for the rest of my life."

"Damn, Ben. You turned sixteen, like, only two months ago."

"No shit. You think I want to be in so deep I can't breathe?"

"I get that. Especially at the beginning when you feel like you're dizzy all the time. It sucks. Who are we talking about? Someone I know?"

I can't say it, but I have to. Maybe I should get off the bed and move across the room. Maybe I should hide in the bathroom and phone it in. Maybe I need to grow a pair.

"Lilli."

Dare literally shudders. "The fuck?"

"One day she's Lilli, one of the Vandenberg kids we've grown up with our whole lives. The next day she's mine, and I'm looking at her in her cute two-piece with those long fuckin' legs, and I'm ready to kill any guy who even glances at her."

My brother wraps his hand around his forehead like he's holding his brain inside his skull. "Does she know?"

"Technically, no."

"Technically? What the fuck does that mean?"

"I haven't said anything to her. I haven't touched her. We haven't talked alone. We haven't texted. Talked on the phone. Sent smoke signals. But I know she knows." I let out a three-part sigh. "We look at each other differently."

"I can imagine how you look at her, you cradle robber. How does she look at you?"

"Like I'm breakfast, lunch, and dinner, including all snacks in between."

"Well, shit. Hearts are in play, huh?"

"Yep. And you gotta know, I have absolutely no intention of taking this anywhere until she's ready."

"Man, it sounds like she thinks she's ready right fuckin' now."

"Yeah, well, that's not going to happen. She turns fifteen in March, and I'm pretty sure she can't go out on dates until she's sixteen, but I think Aunt Amy and Uncle Jonas will allow me to go over to the house. Which is what I want. Adult supervision is required until she's sixteen."

"Until then?"

I know what he's asking, and I'm even less comfortable talking about this part of what I'm going through than I've been about the rest. And I'm so uncomfortable with everything I've told him so far, I feel like hurling.

"I'm hers. I won't violate that."

"Tough road, brother."

"Soccer, baseball, cold showers, and I've decided to start running five miles a day."

"I wanna say this is the 'it sucks' part of being who we are, but I think it's kinda special, ya know?"

"Yeah. And now more than ever, I'm glad I started getting laid young and got my fair share or else by next year I'd be suffering from testicular torsion."

Dare busts out laughing. "I can't believe you remember all that stuff Dad lectured us about. The hundreds of ways our balls and dicks can get fucked up."

"I take wearing a cup seriously. I wear it for the games and practice."

"Surfing?"

"Hell, yeah."

Dare shakes his head. "So only your toes hang loose."

"You better believe it."

"Only you, Ben. Only you would fall so young for someone even younger and make the whole thing seem, what's the word… Gallant. It's gonna be a long haul, but I'm happy for you. She's smart and sweet and really fuckin' pretty."

"Yeah."

"You gonna tell Mom and Dad?"

"I have to. Anything leaks, shit will fly. I don't want that for them or Aunt Amy and Uncle Jonas."

"You got that right."

"I'm thinking I'll text them and ask if we can talk before dinner."

"They'll be glad you're reaching out and manning up. Big points, Ben."

"I hope so."

"You gonna tell Sam?"

"Fuck no."

"Probably best for now. But don't wait too long. Her birthday is when?" Dare does some quick mental math. "Shit. Only three months away."

"Yeah. No matter what I say, Sam's gonna lose his shit."

"You need me for backup, I'm there."

"Thanks, brother. I'm hoping a lifetime of being his best friend will count for something."

"On the one hand, Sam being a man-whore gives him less solid ground to stand on. But, on the other hand, who better than him to know what's at stake?"

"And you were doing so well up until now."

Dare laughs. "It'll be all right, man. You won't let it be anything else."

Since Dare isn't one to blow smoke, I'm going to hang on to that like a lifeline.

***

I sent the text to Mom and Dad's group text. I learned early on: You don't tell only one of them anything important. They're a team. Everything that happens in our family, they deal with together. Not that we would've tried, but they wouldn't've allowed any of us to leverage one of them against the other.

The little everyday things, yeah, we text them individually. If it's me going to the store for Mom, I'll text only her if I need to check on substitution products. Same goes if it's only Dad-related. Like him going with me to get new tires for my car. I know what I'm doing, but the salespeople see a teenager, and they don't give me the kind of deals Dad's able to negotiate.

A half hour before we're supposed to meet everyone at the restaurant for dinner, I'm in Mom and Dad's bungalow, standing next to the little round table in the corner.

Even though I'm pretty much the same height as my dad, he still wraps his elbow around my neck and makes me bend my head so he can kiss the top of it. When I was a little kid, I loved when he did that, and the sentiment hasn't changed even though I'm far from little anymore.

Mom's a hugger. She wraps her arms around my waist and squeezes, which is my signal to bend down and kiss her cheek.

I'm glad I was raised with a lot of affection. All my family is the same way, and that includes Aunt Amy and Uncle Jonas. I've been to some of my teammates' houses, and their parents are so stiff, it's like they'll break if they engage in any physical contact.

"So what's up, son?"

Dad's got three sons, but when he's speaking to me and says "son"—and I know this is true for Dare and Isai too—it makes my chest puff out. He's proud I'm his son, and he has no problem letting me know how he feels.

"I guess the best way to start is to say, you know how we are."

"How who is, specifically?" Mom asks.

"The Di Caros."

"All of us? Some of us? Less than some of us?" Mom likes super-detailed specifics. She's a computer nerd.

"All of us born into the family. You by extension, me by blood."

She smiles and looks at Dad. "Did you know I'm an extension?"

Dad grins in a way meant only for Mom, and I know he's not gonna say what he's thinking. At least, not in front of me. "You're the other half of me. Some might say that's an extension."

"Was he always this slick?" I ask Mom.

She nods. "Always. Something to aspire to."

It'd come in handy right now. "Right. So."

"So. 'You know how we are' is how you opened this conversation," she says. "To what are you referring?"

"How Di Caros fall in love. They fall only once, and when they do, that's it for life."

Dad smiles. "A good family trait to have."

"Well, it sure worked out for you guys." They grin at each other. "See. You're making my point."

"All right, Bennie," Mom says. "We're going to let you off the hook, though you're doing a good job of laying the ground work. This is about Lilli, right?"

My mother is a witch. No lie. She knows and sees things, and I swear, I don't know how she finds out all the shit she has stored in her head. But if you don't respect her witchy ways, she'll drop the whammy on you, and you're fucked.

"Ah, yeah."

"Don't look so surprised," she tells me. "Lilli's your Aunt Amy's oldest girl. You have to know she's keeping a close eye on her teenage daughter."

"Okay. I get that. But we haven't said anything, done anything… I mean, I didn't even know what I'm telling you until two days ago."

"A testament to the density of the teenage boy's brain." Mom laughs. "Lilli knew her mind before you did. Amy's been watching, and she understood what she saw. We've been waiting for you to catch on."

Whoa. Lilli's been into me for a while and I missed it? I can't believe it. But I can. Sort of. But I can't deal with that right now. I've got to get to the bottom line.

"Um, well, here's the thing. No matter how we feel, she's too young. I know I'm going to have to wait to, ah, you know, date her. But I thought, maybe, when she turns fifteen, Uncle Jonas and Aunt Amy would be okay with me going over to, you know, hang out with Lilli."

Dad smiles. "Son, I'm proud of you. It's tough to fall when you're so young, but you've got a good head on your shoulders, and I know you'll be respectful to Lilli and won't disappoint Aunt Amy, Uncle Jonas, or us."

Now who's throwing down? My dad just sewed it up in a couple of sentences. Maybe Mom's witchy stuff's rubbed off on him. And no, I don't want to think about how that might've come about.

Well, since it's all out in the open… "I think Sam's going to want to kill me."

Dad leans in. "I think you may be right." He pauses as I wince. "But, once he sees how you are with Lilli, he'll come around. One thing he'll know for sure is *you*. You've been best friends since day one. He'll get past the obvious big brother stuff, and he'll be glad it's you. He knows the kind of person you are, and he'll want that for his sister."

"I hope so."

Mom pats my hand. "Count on it. But recognize it'll be tense and rocky between you two for a while." I nod. "Okay. Let's go to dinner. I'm famished."

Dad smiles, takes Mom's hand, and walks her out the door. After I'm out on the porch, he's still holding Mom's hand while he locks up.

"I got one more thing before we go."

"Okay," Dad says.

I look at their interlaced fingers. "How do you keep it—"

"Fresh? Alive?" Mom asks.

I nod.

"Every time I look at your mother, I see the person I fell in love with and *know* I wouldn't be who I am and where I am without her."

Mom gets on her toes and kisses Dad's cheek. "Ditto," Mom tells Dad. Then she turns to me and says, "It doesn't hurt to be creative."

I must be wearing my shock because they both start laughing as they walk toward the restaurant.

CHAPTER SEVEN

Drunk in Love

Dare

Dare: Where are you?

Hannah: The garage.

Dare: Because?

Hannah: I'm looking for my cross-country skis.

Dare: Are you going to the mountains?

Hannah: No.

Dare: I'm checking the weather. It's not snowing there.

Hannah: I know that.

Dare: Then why are you looking for your cross-country skis?

Hannah: I thought I'd take them to the beach and try them out there.

Dare: Because?

Hannah: I want to know if they'll make the shooshing sound in the sand.

Dare: Stop looking for the skis. Get in the car, drive to JFK, and get on a plane and come down here right now.

Hannah: Let's pretend I say yes. I've got to go inside and pack. How will I explain that?

Dare: Forget about packing. There are stores here with everything you need. Bathing suits, sarongs, jeans, shorts, tank tops, and flip flops. The hotel supplies the towels, soap, and shampoo, and I'll supply the love and fun.

Hannah: You always make everything sound so easy.

Dare: Because sometimes it is. And when it's not, we have each other to make it better.

Hannah: And what do I say to them when I disappear?

Dare: Text them after you've boarded the plane and tell them where you're going, that my folks are here, and tell them when you'll be back. You're eighteen years old. You don't need their permission to live your life.

Hannah: They're going to bombard me with guilt.

Dare: Not if you turn off your phone.

Hannah: When I get back they'll be twice as bad.

Dare: As opposed to right now when you're looking for your skis to go shooshing on the sand because you'll do anything to get out of that house.

Hannah: I'm not as strong as you.

Dare: Yeah you are. You don't want them to see it because then they'll know you're your own person, which isn't a crime, baby. It's time for you to spread your wings and enjoy life.

Hannah: Are you sure about this?

Dare: Totally. You have your passport?

Hannah: Yeah. It's in my bag.

Dare: Perfect.

Hannah: What will your parents say?

Dare: They can't wait to meet you. They'll be happy you're here.

Hannah: Where will I stay?

Dare: With me.

Hannah: They won't freak about us being together.

Dare: Baby, they already know we're together. We'll be in our own space, and we'll be with the fam when we feel like it.

Hannah: What about the ticket?

Dare: It'll be waiting for you at the airport. Get your ass in the car right now and drive to JFK. I'll take care of everything and text you the airline and flight number.

Hannah: You sure?

Dare: Baby, get your fine ass in the car right now.

Hannah: This is crazy.

Dare: Are you in the car yet?

Hannah: Yeah.

Dare: Buckle in, drive safe, and I'll see you soon.

Hannah: Have I told you how much I miss you.

Dare: Yeah, baby. And I miss you, and you know it.

Hannah: See you soon.

Dare: Thank fuck.

When I book the flight, I allow for plenty of time for her to make the plane. If there's traffic, driving to JFK could take three hours. If it doesn't, she'll have time to talk to me while she's waiting at the gate.

I'm not telling anyone she's on her way until I know she's picked up the ticket and is on the plane.

***

Dare: Where are you guys?

Mom & Dad Group Text: We're having lunch on the beach. Why?

Dare: I need the car.

M&DGT: Because?

Dare: I'm going to Liberia Airport to pick up Hannah.

M&DGT: Oh, honey. I'm so glad.

Dare: Where on the beach are you?

M&DGT: Directly in line with the girls' bungalow.

Dare: K.

Ten minutes later I'm standing in front of a huge round table with a huge umbrella, saying "hi" to all the parents as my dad hands me the keys to the rental car.

"We can't wait to meet her," Aunt Amy tells me. And before I respond, she goes on to say, "We know she's shy, and we won't overwhelm her, but if you need us, we're here for the both of you."

One of the reasons none of us ever get too wild, in too much trouble, or engage in too much assholery is because every single one of these people are, and have been, there for all fourteen of us kids no matter whose child we are. Aside from the constant support, they're really good at laying on subtle guilt, which means none of us want to disappoint them.

Sometimes having a large, interfering family is a pain in the ass. But most of the time, it's fun and comfortable, and all the kids know we have a big safety net to protect us.

I say, "Thanks," to Aunt Amy and give the group a low wave.

As I'm walking away, my dad calls, "Wait up." I stop, and he hands me a disc swipe and says, "For your bungalow."

"I was heading over to the front desk to take care of it myself."

Dad smiles and says, "Did I ever tell you what my father did when your mom was leaving Fiddler's Rest to move back east to be with me?"

I shake my head. "I don't think so."

"She'd come out of taking her last test and was walking to the parking lot when, out of nowhere, my father appeared. She'd never met him before, but there he was, making it clear since she was mine, she was his too. He offered her a ride back to Providence in his plane."

"Sounds like *Nonno*. Bet he liked her right away 'cause Mom doesn't back down from anyone or anything."

"Yeah. They understand each other on a level most never reach with him."

"I get what you're telling me, but I already know that's how you and Mom feel. I knew it would be how you would feel before I even talked to you."

Dad wraps his arm around my neck and yanks me against him as he kisses the top of my head. "Be happy, *Dario mio*."

I hug him hard, then walk to the rental.

***

Hannah is lying on my chest, her legs tangled with mine. I'm holding her dark brown hair in a bunch at the back of her head. It's layered, so I miss as much hair as I gather.

"Tell me again, how many people are going to be at dinner?" she mumbles into my neck.

Her plane landed on time, and the moment she saw me, she burst into tears. She's super sensitive, and her fuckin' parents use that against her, which pisses me the hell off, but I can't let how I feel show. She's conflicted enough, I don't need to make it worse.

After she calmed down, she told me, "I did what you said and turned off my phone after I texted them." She dug into her bag and pulled out the phone. "You take it. This way I won't be tempted to check what I'm sure is four hundred texts, each getting progressively worse and more threatening."

I took the phone and shoved it in my pocket.

Thankfully, on the ride back, she was so taken by the scenery, I was able to steer the conversation to everything that's been happening with the fam since we got here, including our twenty-five-person dinner every night.

"Twenty-five," I tell her. "All eleven adults sit together at one table—"

"Eleven?"

"Uncle Jonas's mother, Elaine, comes along to keep an eye on the girls, who are too young to be in a bungalow on their own. She's been doing it for years and deserves a medal for Lei-lei alone."

"I know you told me before, but I can't keep them all straight. Which one's Lei-lei?"

"Uncle Jonas and Aunt Amy's youngest kid. She's ten. Her real name's Helen, but since she's been a baby, everyone calls her Lei-lei. She's wicked smart, but it's like she's perpetually cranky. She argues about everything."

"Like unhappy arguing?"

"No. She enjoys dishing out verbal abuse. It's her version of a contact sport."

Hannah giggles. "Sounds like a handful."

"Totally."

"So, the eleven adults sit together, and everyone else is at another table?"

"Yeah. Lia and Alex sit at one end of the table with me, Misha, Rafe, and Luca. Though it's not official, the rest of the guys sit in descending age order in the middle across from each other, and the four girls sit at the other end all huddled together."

"So we'll just say hi to your parents and the rest of the adults, then we'll sit with Lia and them?"

"Baby, trust me. You have nothing to be nervous about. You already know Bennie and Sam. Everyone else is happy you're here, and they can't wait to meet you. I know there's a lot of us, and it seems like it'll be overwhelming, but we've known each other forever, and we're chill. Especially here. We're in paradise, baby, enjoying our vacay. Pretty much all we do is eat, surf, swim, play b-ball, lie on the beach and shoot the shit, or hang at our bungalows."

"Okay. But I'm wearing the sundress tonight."

I smile. She's invested in making a good impression. "Wear whatever you want."

***

Hannah spent too long getting ready. I know her insecurities are rooted in the way her parents raised her, and recently have been compounded by all the family shit that's been swirling for the past year. It's totally fucked up. Her brother, who I sort of know—he was a couple of years ahead of me in school—is an arrogant prick who thinks his shit doesn't stink. Her parents made him that way by treating him like the sun shines out of his ass, while they treat Hannah as less than in everything. Like she isn't as good as him, when, in fact, she's smarter, more talented, kinder, and way more decent than he'll ever be.

I can't undo what her parents have done, but I can, and will, make sure she knows how special she is. Not only to me, but to my fam. It's impossible to erase someone else's shitty behavior, but I have it in me to show Hannah that the rest of her tomorrows will be filled with love and support. The first hurdle: get her to go to Brown with me.

We're walking hand in hand through a landscape thick with palm trees wrapped in little twinkling lights. It's a little after seven-thirty, so it's dark and we have to stay on the lit pathways to see where we're going. Those lights on the palm trees don't throw off big lumens.

As we enter the restaurant, I can't help but shake my head when Mom sees me. Her smile is bright and wide, as is Aunt Sofia's, Aunt Ro's, Aunt Amy's, Aunt Theresa's, and Elaine's. No doubt Mom and Dad briefed all the adults about me and Hannah. Some people would mind having so many family members up in their business, but all us kids were raised to expect it.

Sofia and Ro are my dad's sisters. They're blood. Amy became a Di Caro when she was seven—the year she and Sofia became besties, and when *Nonno* adopted her into his heart. Once there, Amy was a full Di Caro in every way that mattered. Theresa saved Sofia's life, for real. She stepped in front of a bullet meant for Sofia. To this day, *Nonno* says there's nothing he won't do for Theresa. Another Di Caro, more or less. Elaine is Amy's mother-in-law—so another Di Caro, more or less.

Dad's best friend and business partner is Jonas. Matt and Collin are my dad's brothers-in-law, and Ethan is Theresa's man, so that makes him ours. And all their children are our cousins by blood or by extension. It's a lot, but not really. We're our own tribe, and tonight, although I didn't tell her this exactly, Hannah is being inducted in.

I guide her to the one end of the table where my parents are sitting. "Mom, Dad, this is Hannah."

With anyone else, they'd get up and hug her. But they understand Hannah's shy and tentative, so they stay seated but ask innocuous questions: "How was your flight?" and "Have you been in the water yet?"

As I introduce Hannah around the table, she gets more of the same. "Do you surf?" "Did Dare tell you there are tennis courts, pickleball courts, basketball courts, and volleyball nets are set up on the beach?"

Most of her answers are short, but she's polite and sweet, and she blushes when Elaine tells her, "Such a pretty sundress. That deep peach goes great with your complexion."

At the kids' table, there are two empty seats directly across from Misha and Luca. Lia and Alex are sitting at the head of the table, Bennie's sitting next to Hannah, and Sam's next to Luca. My fam's made sure Hannah is surrounded by people she knows and has the oldest kids all around her. Fuckin' brilliant.

Within minutes after we sit, waiters bring out pitchers of the house lemonade and iced tea. A pitcher of beer is placed at our end of the table, as is a bottle of champagne. I look up to see my mom watching, and I smile. Mom doesn't miss a trick.

Another wave of waiters comes out with huge platters, tureens, and baskets filled with grilled fish, *rondón*—a seafood coconut stew—veggie hash, rice and beans, tamales wrapped in banana leaves, and *pan casero*, rolls that are kind of sweet.

Hannah leans into me and asks, "No one orders from the menu?"

"I'm sure the other patrons do, but we're here every night, and serving both tables family-style with the daily specials, a few staples, and our faves is easier on the staff. We've been coming here for years, so they know what we like, and each year they introduce us to new dishes. You'll see. There'll be almost nothing left by the time everyone's passed around all the food."

While we stuff our faces, conversation flows easily, and while not obvious, I notice everyone's making an effort to include Hannah, who slowly opens up and joins in. It took her a while to feel safe with me, but once she did, she began telling me everything. With new people, she takes her time warming up, though she's better than she used to be. This group is so close-knit, weaving someone into our fabric doesn't take much, as long as the newbie is brought in by a tribe member.

After the dirty dishes, empty platters, tureens, and baskets are taken away, the staff brings out clean plates, more pitchers of lemonade and iced tea, as well as locally harvested coffee. Tonight's desserts are: *prestiños*, a syrupy fried dough; *cajetas*, a nougat topped with coconut and peanuts; and coconut *flan*.

Hannah's blinking rapidly at the second wave of food. "This is unbelievable. There was so much dinner, and it was so good, I couldn't help but taste everything. There's no way I have room for dessert. Does anyone?"

"Yeah," I say as I load up my plate with two of everything in case she changes her mind. "We burn it off surfing or playing b-ball." I grin. "We're growing boys."

Bennie and Sam crack up. "Yeah, Hans." Sam rolls up his t-shirt sleeve and makes the strongman biceps bulge. "Need to keep up my strength."

She shakes her head while giving him a bright smile.

The girls, who'd said hello when we came to the table, now migrate over to us. Lilli stands behind Bennie, and I bite the inside of my mouth as I watch Sam narrow his eyes as she curls her fingers around the back of his chair. Thankfully, he can't see her brushing her index fingers on Bennie's back. My brother is so fucked it isn't even funny.

"So." Lei-lei pushes her way to stand between Hannah and my chair, then looks at Hannah. "You and Dare, huh?"

"You must be Lei-lei," Hannah says.

"The one and only," Lei-lei sasses.

"Why don't you take your one-and-only butt back down to the other end of the table?" Though framed as a question, Sam's not suggesting.

Lei-lei continues talking to Hannah. "I don't pay him any attention. He's such a man-whore, his brain is clouded with testosterone. I'm pretty sure he has no idea what he's saying most of the time."

Hannah leans over the table and gives me wide eyes. I shake my head and chuckle.

"Yo, Pip," Luca calls. "*A basta.*"

Most of the guys call Lei-lei "Pip," short for pipsqueak. She hates it as much as she hates being dismissed, which is what Luca's doing by telling her "Enough" in Italian.

Lilli, who's calm and steady, turns to her sister and says, "C'mon, Lei-lei. I see Mimi is getting ready to go." Lilli turns to Liv and Nic with a pleading expression.

"Yeah," Nic says. "I call dibs on the door hammock."

Lei-lei shouts, "Dibs on the other hammock."

The tag-team works, and the girls get Lei-lei to head out.

"Poor Isai," Bennie says. "He's the only one who'll be around when Pip starts high school."

"Only one year, asshole," Isai says. "I'll be a senior. Which means I'll have nothing to do with her aggravating ass."

Everyone laughs. Even Hannah.

CHAPTER EIGHT

Sweetest Taboo

Bennie

I'm sitting on the top step to Dare and Hannah's bungalow, knowing my brother is not going to be happy to see me. But I need advice, and I'm sure as fuck not going to talk about this to my parents.

Hannah's tucked under Dare's arm, and he's whispering something in her ear that makes her look up at him with a knowing smile. Yeah. My brother's definitely not going to be happy to see me.

Dare glances toward the bungalow, and his brows go up. He must be telling Hannah I'm here 'cause he lifts his chin in my direction.

"Hey, Bennie," she says in a whisper-soft voice.

My brother found a really nice girl. She's sweet, and she's as into him as he is her. I don't doubt their future happiness. He's got that locked down tight. Shit, he wanted her here, and she's on the next flight down.

"Yo, Hans. Sorry to crash your evening."

"It's okay. I'll go inside so you and Dare can talk."

"No, no," I tell her. "Stay." I sigh. "I'm gonna need all the help I can get."

Her gaze darts to Dare, and he nods. We move up to the porch and arrange the chairs so we can see each other.

Before I can say a word, Dare tells me, "I saw."

"So did Sam," Hannah adds.

Shit. "He saw the finger move?"

"I don't think so," she says.

"Nah," Dare confirms. "He saw her curl her hands around your chair, but no way he could see her brushing her fingers on your back."

I shake my head in disbelief. "Why did she do that?"

"Because you're taking too long to make a move."

Hannah lets out a squeak. Dare stifles a chuckle, and I'm stunned, shocked, and speechless.

"Lilli, honey," Dare says softly, "you shouldn't be walking around at night by yourself."

She turns and points. "I'm two bungalows away, and Mimi watched me walk over here. I told her I wanted to talk to Hannah, and she said okay, but I should take my phone, and she'd watch me walk over. She also told me to have you and Hannah walk me back."

"Okay." Dare nods. "You're here. What's up?"

She glances at me and scowls. I didn't even know Lilli could scowl. "He's what's up. I figured Hannah would have some insight since she's with you."

"Same gene pool, different personalities," Dare says.

I point to myself. "I'm sitting right here."

"Yeah, well, I'm standing right here"—Lilli points to herself—"and you haven't addressed the issue."

I have to keep myself from shouting. "The issue is you're too young."

"I'll be fifteen in three months." She says it as if she's telling me she'll be twenty in three months.

"That's still two years too young. The age of consent in New York is seventeen."

She walks up the last two steps and stares. "That didn't seem to deter you up 'til now," she shoots back.

I'm sure as fuck not going to talk to her about my sex life. "Excuse me? Did I promise you something I forgot about?"

"Ben," Dare says in a low, warning tone.

Lilli's about five feet away from me, standing on the porch with her arms crossed over her long-sleeve tee, giving me what my *nonna* calls the hairy eyeball.

"It's okay, Dare. He's being an ass." She returns her gaze to me. "Believe me. It's not the first time."

Who is this girl? She's sure as hell not the Lilli I know. "Come again?"

"Let's go back to the promises you made but seem to've forgotten."

I make a rolling motion with my hand for her to have her say.

"You liked the ruffly two-piece, but your tongue nearly fell out of your mouth over the crop top."

Okay. Maybe I wasn't as guarded as I thought I was. And I had told Dare we looked at each other differently, but I damn sure didn't make any promises.

"If there was a promise made from admiring a bathing suit, about fifty other guys made a promise too."

She grins an *I got you* grin, then says, "I'm so glad you brought up those other guys since that's part of the promise you made."

I'm baffled. "How's that?"

"Every time one of those guys stared, winked, or started to come near me, you gave them a *I'll rip your eyes out of their sockets* look."

Dare barked out a laugh, and Hannah giggled.

Okay. I'd admitted that to Dare too. But I'm sure I kept all that in my head. I don't remember making any noises, faces, or remarks. Shit. I'm not getting anywhere dodging her. I need to take a different tack.

"Lil. What do you want from me?"

"Honesty."

"How am I being dishonest?"

"By keeping what you feel for me from me."

I stand, take her hand for the first time since I've known she's my "one," and I sit on the top step and pull her down next to me. I angle my body to face her, and she does the same.

"I'm not telling you because there's nothing we can do about it. Not for years. If, after you turn fifteen, your parents are okay with me coming over to hang out, then I'll be there as often as I can. But that's it until you're sixteen and we can go out on dates."

"Until you go away to college."

"Yeah. But I'll be home for the holidays for at least three weeks." I squeeze her hand. "If what we have is real, then we'll be fine."

"So basically, you're telling me we've got to wait fifteen months before you'll even kiss me?"

She's killing me. Sitting inches away, our knees almost touching, her long legs on display in her cutoff jean shorts, and wearing sweet old-school Keds and a white long-sleeve tee. She looks like a dream and is acting like a siren. I have no choice: I nod.

"That's thinking like people did a hundred years ago."

"Lil. That's thinking like a guy who respects you and your family. Don't make me out to be dishonest because I do."

She holds my gaze, and I sigh. She needs more. "If, in any way, I conveyed a promise to you, this is me keeping that promise at the same time promising our families that I'll do the right thing."

She drops her head, and I feel like I kicked her in the gut.

Hannah, who hasn't said a word since Lilli got here, comes over and crouches beside Lilli. "You wanted to talk to me. Get my opinion. You still want that?"

Lilli nods.

"Okay. Dare and Bennie have different personality types, but they have the same set of values. Dare'd do the same thing Bennie's doing, and it's one of the reasons I love him. It doesn't matter to me who Dare went out with before me and what he did with them. He didn't give them any promises, and they knew what they were getting into.

"I believe you believe Bennie made promises to you through actions, not words. And though I have no idea what Bennie's feeling, I can guess." Hannah pushes her index finger against Lilli's shoulder. "You're it for him. The one.

"He's probably kicking himself because the timing stinks, but these things don't happen on a timetable. So, knowing you're too young"—Lilli opens her mouth, but Hannah keeps talking—"and you are too young, he's doing the right thing. You may not think you're too young, and you may have deep feelings for Bennie, but fourteen was four years ago for me, and I was nowhere near ready for the weight of being in a committed relationship that is heading toward my forever."

Hannah looks at me and smiles. "I've known Bennie for a couple of years. He's really smart, and because he's in an accelerated program, he's been in a couple of classes with me. He's a good guy." Hannah shifts her gaze to Lilli. "He wouldn't lie to you, but he will protect you. I know it's not what you want right now, but it's what you need."

She pats Lilli's shoulder, then stands. "Give me your phone." Lilli pulls her phone out of her back pocket, opens the screen, and hands it to Hannah. "While I'm here, I don't have a phone, so if you need me, call Dare. I'm putting his and my number in your contacts. When we're back at school, text me your schedule, and we'll find time to be together. Okay?"

Lilli nods, and Hannah starts tapping on the phone, then hands it back to Lilli, who pockets it and grabs my hand. "We can call each other, right?"

"Yeah."

"Text."

"Yeah."

She looks at her lap and says, "I better get back before Mimi starts freaking."

"I'll walk you," I say. Then I give her hand a gentle tug, and after she's standing, I bring the back of her hand to my lips, which I press lightly against her soft skin.

We don't even take a step down when something slams into me so hard I go flying and hit the door of the bungalow with my head and shoulders.

"I knew it," Sam shouts. "I fuckin' knew it." He's yanking me up, and I'm seeing stars floating in my vision and little else. "You muthafucka." His fist cracks against my jaw, and I go down again.

Lilli's beside me, crying, "Oh, Bennie. Talk to me."

I hear Dare screaming, "What the fuck, Sam? Hannah and I are right here with them."

"So you're okay with him kissing my FOURTEEN-YEAR-OLD SISTER?" Sam bellows.

I hear a scuffle, but I'm too dizzy to lift my head. I hope Sam isn't trying to take on Dare. He'll kick Sam's ass into tomorrow.

"He kissed the back of her hand, you moron."

I try to right myself, and Lilli helps me by putting the weight of her body against my shoulder. I place my hand on my throbbing head and feel wet near my ear. I move my hand in front of my face, and Lilli gasps, then she's crying louder.

My vision is blurry, but I'm pretty sure I see blood. I bring my fingers near my nose, and yeah, it smells like blood.

"Dare," I rasp.

"Dare," Lilli screams.

I feel my brother beside me. "Hang on, Ben. I'm calling Dad, and I'll tell him to bring Uncle Jonas and Aunt Amy."

***

Dad and Uncle Jonas are carrying me into Dare and Hannah's bungalow. I hear someone flapping something. A shirt? Then I'm lowered onto what I think is their bed, but I'm kind of disoriented.

"Here," Dad says. "Take this into the bathroom, and after you wash your hands, pat them dry and put the Betadine ointment on all your knuckles and other lacerated skin. When you come out, I'll wrap your hands."

I guess he's talking to Sam. Asshole. Talk about act first, ask questions later.

"Ben," Dad says softly. "Open your eyes for me, son."

I try, but my head is killing me, and the light's too bright. "Head hurts," I whisper.

"Okay. Hold tight. The ambulance should be here any minute. We're going to a private hospital about twenty minutes away. They have the facilities to do an MRI. I'll be in the ambulance with you, and everyone else will follow in their cars. You understand?"

"Yeah," I whisper.

"Stay with me and keep squeezing my finger."

I do as he asks, and it seems like no time has gone by and I'm in the ambulance and Dad is right there with me.

***

MRI machines are fuckin' noisy. My head hurts enough. I could've done without all that banging metal-against-metal sound.

***

Hospitals smell. But at least the light in the room is low, and my head isn't throbbing so bad anymore.

"Ben," Dad says. "Hey, son. How are you feeling?"

"Better than...yesterday?"

"Yeah. Last night. Can you see me?"

"You're a bit blurry, but the light isn't killing me anymore, so that's a plus."

Mom leans over and runs her fingers through my hair. "You look better. Are you nauseous?"

I take inventory. "Everything below my shoulders feels fine. My right shoulder hurts, and my head isn't great, but I can talk closer to a normal level. How do I sound?"

"Like my Bennie," she says.

"So what's the diagnosis?" I ask Dad.

"We had them do an MRI and a CT. No evidence of brain bleeds. We'll have them done again in a couple of days. Symptomology indicates a moderate concussion. You have a persistent headache, some confusion and dizziness, and fatigue. We're going to get you up after lunch to see if you have problems with balance and/or coordination. I don't expect you will, and if that's the case, you'll be discharged by four this afternoon."

"How's Sam?"

"Kicking his own ass so hard, it doesn't seem like we're going to have to do or say anything to make him feel any worse than he does."

"Aunt Amy and Uncle Jonas?"

"Upset," Mom says. "Pissed off at Sam. Worried about Lilli, who hasn't stopped crying. She blames herself for going over to Dare and Hannah's."

"Well, that's stupid. She had no way of knowing I'd be there."

"Honey." Mom puts her hand in mine. "Affairs of the heart rarely make sense. Until they do."

"Great," I groan. "Cryptic. Always helpful."

Dad chuckles. "Yeah. He's feeling better."

***

Dad insists I ride back to the bungalow in an ambulance. He wants me to rest another day. He's the MD, and I'm his kid. Not worth an argument.

Misha switches rooms with me so I can have a room on the ground floor. Easier access to the kitchen and porch, and Misha's room has its own bathroom. Mom and Dad are hanging on the porch.

Close, but not hovering. I've been in the room for about an hour, propped up in bed, when the fam parade begins.

Aunt Amy's carrying a fruit basket, and Uncle Jonas comes in, sits on the side of the bed, and says, "We're not going to apologize for his behavior. That's on him. But we are sorry you got hurt."

"Thanks. I know you are." Uncle Jonas nods. "I'll wait a while to let Sam off the hook, but if it's okay with you, I want to see Lilli so she knows I'm going to be fine."

"She told us everything," Aunt Amy says. "You must know we trust you implicitly. If you guys go the distance, we couldn't ask for a better person to be our daughter's life partner."

Well, all fuckin' right. One for the win column.

Aunt Ro and Uncle Collin visit along with Aunt Sofia and Uncle Matt. They tell me *Nonno* and *Nonna* plan to come stay with us for a week after we're back in New York. *Nonna* will cook up a storm, and *Nonno* will pass judgment on everything and everybody.

Aunt Theresa and Uncle Ethan come with Lia and Alex, who catch me up on all the Calapiano family news. There's the east coast Calapianos who are in Connecticut, except for Aunt Theresa and Uncle Ethan, who live in a Boston suburb, and the California Calapianos, who own a huge vineyard and are vintners.

After they leave, Mom and Dad come in and tell me they're off duty for a few hours, and Dare, Hannah, and Lilli are coming over with dinner.

All the visiting has made me tired, and I ask Dad if it's okay if I take a nap. He arranges for Luca and Rafe to take shifts to check on me, and I'm half asleep before they leave.

***

"Is he breathing?" I hear Lilli's panicked voice ask.

I feel something under my nose, and I smack it away. Dare cracks up and says, "Breathing and ornery."

I open my eyes to see Hannah sitting on one side of my bed, Lilli on the other. Hannah smiles, then says, "Dare and I are going to help Luca, Rafe, Isai, and Artie set up for dinner. We'll come back to get you and Lilli when everything's ready."

"Thanks," I tell her.

"Good to see you, brother." Dare bends down and whispers, "Don't ever do that to me again."

I grin up at him. "I'll try."

In his Yoda voice, he says, "There is no try." Then he slaps my leg before he leaves.

Lilli is biting her lower lip and looking at me from under her lashes.

"Come here, Lil." She gets up, climbs up on the bed, and sits beside me. "I'm fine. I have a concussion. By the time we get on the plane to go home, I'll be all healed."

"Are you in pain?" she whispers.

"My head hurts a little. Like when you have a cold. Dad says the ache should dissipate in a couple of days when I'm going back to have the imaging done again. It's not required, but Dad's being extra careful."

"I'm glad he is. I was so worried."

"Now listen to me, Lil, and by that, I mean take in what I'm telling you. None of this is your fault. You went to talk to Hannah. You had no idea I would be there. 'Kay?"

"I hear what you're saying, but I'm not good with poofing my feelings away." I lower my brows. "But," she adds with a sigh, "I promise to work on it."

"Good. Next thing. You're not responsible for your brother's behavior. Sam's always had a short fuse. Great guy, hair-trigger temper. You're his sister, so you know what I'm saying is the truth."

"I know," she says. "He lost it, and there wasn't even a reason to lose it, and he could've hurt you more than he hurt you, which is terrible enough."

"Lil. I'm going to be all right. You think my dad won't do everything in his power to make sure I'm a hundred percent?"

"I know he will."

"Right. So we agree about Sam, but this is the crazy-good thing: it'll never happen again. Not when it comes to us. I knew he'd go nutso when he found out, and I hoped it wouldn't be for at least another year. But since this went down now, it's all good. He and I will find a way to get back to where we were. He's been my best friend since before I can remember. I have no intention of losing that. You with me?"

She gives me a sweet little smile. "I'm with you."

Hannah stands in my doorway. "Dinner's ready. You need any help getting up?"

"Nah. I'm slow, but I'm steady."

"Okay."

Lilli gets off the bed and says, "How about I spot you?"

I tilt my head at the bathroom. "Give me a minute."

"Ben. You have all my time, and always will."

CHAPTER NINE

Everlasting

Gio

"I've never been that scared in my entire life," I tell Nat. "Sitting in the ambulance, all I could think was how lucky we've been. In the most impossible way, you and I found each other, and nothing has ever come close to what it means to having you love me, and for me to love you." She snuggles against me and throws her leg over my thigh. "We followed our career paths, and look where they led us. The trajectory and our accomplishments are amazing."

"They are," she whispers. "Totally phenomenal."

"You had three easy pregnancies. We have three healthy children who we love and adore, and they make us proud."

"They're the absolute best."

"But until I saw the second set of images today, and conferred with the radiologists here and at home, did I finally pull in a full, deep breath. He's going to be all right."

"He's going to be better than all right. He's going to have a beautiful life. That little girl, she's fierce. She's one of those still waters that run deep. He's going to know the kind of love we've shared, and he's going to enjoy the kind of professional success we've enjoyed. I predict he's going to follow in your footsteps and become a doctor."

"Really? He's never expressed an interest in medicine."

"He's really responsible. Look at how he's handled everything regarding Lilli. And, I think after this episode, he's going to start considering what it means to have your health and how important a good doctor is in helping a person get to a place where they can recapture their good health."

"Dare seems pretty set on becoming a lawyer, and if Bennie chooses medicine, it'd make me all kinds of happy. You think it's too early to think about the path Isai will take?"

"I think our Isai is a dark horse. Quiet and contemplative, he'll wait until he's sure he's found his passion."

"He loves to cook and bake. He's always helping Jonas when he puts together one of his feasts."

"A chef? You've had a lot of talented cooks in your family. It's definitely a possibility."

She stretches like a cat and begins to rub herself against me.

"You feeling frisky, Ace?"

"I could be persuaded."

I roll on top of her as she spreads her legs, creating all sort of opportunities. "Let's see how powerful my persuasiveness still is."

***

Nat's ass is snuggled tight against my groin. Uncharacteristically, she's fallen asleep first. Usually, she knocks me out. But, tonight, even though she didn't say so, I know she was as relieved as I was that our Bennie is going to make a full recovery, and working out the last of her nervousness made her fall asleep earlier than usual.

As I tighten my arm around her waist, the house phone rings. If it's one of our kids, they'd call one of our cells. Same goes for our family. But, after the past few days, I'm taking nothing for granted. I check the time—a little past midnight—then pick up the old-fashioned receiver and listen.

"Doctor Di Caro?"

Nat's sitting up with me, the sleepy completely gone from her face. I put the receiver between us so she can hear.

"Who's asking?"

"Sy Baranski."

"I think you have the wrong number."

"Sy Baranski. Hannah's father."

"How can I help you, Mr. Baranski?"

"Are you aware your son, Dario, has kidnapped my daughter?"

Nat pulls in her lips to keep from laughing.

"Mr. Baranski, that would be impossible. Our son was here in Costa Rica days prior to Hannah's arrival. She came here of her own free will."

"She'd never get a plane and leave us and the country unless he'd inveigled her."

"There was no inveigling. She's eighteen years old. An adult. She can come and go as she pleases."

"Listen here, Di Caro. I know all about your family. Your type of people. I'm contacting the local police here, the local police there, the FBI, and the State Department."

"Please feel free to contact whomever you wish, Mr. Baranski. I bid you a good morning."

"Ho-lee shit." Nat shakes her head. "Dare said they're controlling, manipulative nutters, but I don't think that begins to cover it."

"Clearly." I take the receiver off the hook and disconnect the cord from the base. "It's late. Tomorrow's soon enough to let Dare know about the call."

Nat yawns. "Let's go to sleep, babe. Who knows what tomorrow will bring."

***

Pounding on the door wakes me from a deep sleep.

"What the fuck?" Nat mutters.

"Whoever it is, I bet the Baranski guy's behind it." I pull on my jeans and go to the door and ask, "Who's there?"

"*Lo siento*, Señor Di Caro. It is Raul. The night manager."

I open the door and step onto the porch to see a slim middle-age man in the hotel's uniform of a tropical shirt and khaki pants. He has a nametag on that says "Raul Garcia, Manager."

"What's going on, Raul?"

"A man keeps calling the front desk, and he is yelling angry because you are not picking up your phone."

"I unplugged the phone after I talked to the yelling angry man hours ago."

"Ah, *yo comprendo*. But he tells me he is going to send the police because your son kidnaps his daughter."

I shake my head. If this wasn't such a nightmare for Hannah, it'd be funny. "My son didn't kidnap his daughter. She's an adult who chose to come here." His shoulders slump, and he nods. "I doubt the police will come because a yelling angry man from the U.S. calls them. If they do come, they'll see her passport and know she's an adult."

"*Yo comprendo*. I will tell yelling angry man he needs to stop calling. Your telephone is broken."

"*Bueno*."

Raul sighs and takes off in the direction of the main hotel building.

I open the door to find Nat in her robe, leaning against the wall beside the door. "You get all that?"

"Pretty much."

"Baranski's out of control. I'm thinking we need to talk to Dare and Hannah. It won't be pleasant, but she needs to know what's going on."

"*Yo comprendo*."

I grin and take her back to bed.

***

The next morning we're sitting at a round table on the beach, having breakfast with Theresa and Ethan, who have had just heard the whole Baranski and Raul story, when one of the hotel staff comes to the table and hands me an envelope. I pass it to Nat, knowing Baranski has something to do with whatever's in the envelope.

"This is too fucked for words." Nat hands me the single sheet with scrawly handwriting that says: "Di Caro, tell my adult daughter since she's so attached to your family, you can pay for her college education. Sy Baranski"

I hand the note to Ethan, who takes one look at the handwriting and says, "Oh yeah. World-class nutter." He hands the note to Theresa.

"I feel bad for Hannah on two fronts," Theresa says. "She had to endure growing up with those people, and at her first assertion of independence, they abandon her. I hope it doesn't take her long to realize they did her a favor." Theresa's a shrink. It's good to know she echoes my thoughts.

"No time like the present," Nat says as she takes out her phone. "Dare, honey. Can you and Hannah meet us on the beach?" Nat's listening to Dare. "We've eaten too, but we'd like to talk if you have time." She nods. "Right. We're at a table under an umbrella about twenty feet before the volleyball nets." She smiles. "Sure. Half an hour."

About twenty minutes later, Ethan and Theresa leave, the table is cleared, and our waiter brings a fresh carafe of coffee, fresh plates and utensils, and a basket of *pan casero*. Always good to have fresh bread on the table. Especially this sweet bread, which tastes like cake.

Nat sees Dare and Hannah and waves them over.

They sit, pour coffee, and Dare dives into the *pan casero* at the same time he's looking at us, and I can see him trying to gauge what's going on.

Nat takes the lead, which is best. Every time I replay this shit in my head, I get pissed off.

"So we had a couple of interruptions early this morning."

"Interruptions?" Dare's smart. He's caught on this has something to do with Hannah's folks.

Hannah, who seems to take her cues from him, tilts her head. "Is everything all right?"

"Your father called us around twelve-thirty this morning." Hannah's eyes widen, and her brows go up. "At first he said Dare kidnapped you, but when Gio told him that was impossible, and you're an adult who can go where she wants, he wasn't pleased."

"Did he threaten to sic the cops on you?" Hannah asks while shaking her head.

"The cops, the FBI, and the State Department," I tell her.

"Typical. He thinks he can scare or bully people into doing what he wants. I'm sorry he disturbed you."

"He really upset the night manager, Raul. Gio had unplugged the phone, and when your father couldn't get through, he called the front desk repeatedly. We had a visit from the night manager at about three this morning."

"No shit?" Dare asks.

"No shit," I say.

"I'm so sorry," Hannah rushes to say. "This is humiliating."

"Not for you," Nat tells her. "You didn't do anything wrong, and you weren't the one disturbing us."

"But you were disturbed because of me. He's my father."

"Who's a grown man and knows better. You're not responsible for his behavior," I say.

"We're telling you all this because this note was faxed to the hotel and delivered to us about an hour ago." Nat passes the note to Dare, who makes sure he's close enough for Hannah to see it too.

"What a fuckin' dick," Dare mutters.

"He so is," Hannah says.

Hannah's been here only for a few days, but clearly alone time with Dare has given her a new perspective, or perhaps has allowed her to express herself freely. In any case, it's refreshing to see her coming out of her shell. And good for Dare for seeing who she really is this whole time, even though she'd been battling the pull of her guilt-mongering parents.

"Have I told you the story about how I sold my fancy sports car to pay for your mother's tuition to Brown?"

Dare grins.

I grin back.

And know. My son and future daughter-in-law won't be attending the Air Force Academy. They'll be attending Brown. Together. They'll live together, and Nat and I will pay for both their tuitions.

Because the love a Di Caro has for family is as everlasting as the love a Di Caro has for their "one."

DEEP DIVE

Misty Urban

I never wanted to see Anton Olivier again.

So naturally, he showed up at my hotel. Right before Christmas. Strolling into the big, open-air reception space of the resort as if he owned the place and expected people to prostrate themselves before him like some island deity. Which was what he looked like.

My pulse catapulted into high gear. "They're not supposed to be here." I pulled my assistant, Nic, behind the curved hospitality desk as the band of big, luggage-toting men strutted across the lanai. "We're closed. Who let them in?"

December in the Seychelles meant a balmy eighty degrees every day, so most of the crew wore thin T-shirts or no shirts with their baggy shorts and sandals. Muscles in every shade of brown bulged with the weight of scuba gear and sturdy duffels. They laughed, joked, and clattered into my serene, carefully designed space like typical noisy men, but my gaze homed like a pigeon onto the one in front.

The one with the sunglasses shading eyes I knew were a knock-you-down, steal-your-breath steel blue. The one with sweat glistening on his bare chest, dusted with black hair that defined the lean muscles built by long hours in the water.

He'd shaved the beard he'd worn in France, and the dark stubble sculpted his jaw and cheekbones into sensual art. I swore I could smell him coming, that mix of salt and musk and man that was signature Anton Olivier. So was the confident walk, shoulders thrown back, biceps flexing as he swung his dive bag off his shoulder and set it on the freshly laid reclaimed wood floor.

I knew, as did his crew, no one but Anton Olivier touched his dive bag.

But women touched Anton Olivier all the time.

He was bait, and he was waiting for me to bite.

So said the cocky smile he slanted at me as he sauntered up to my desk. That smile made women all over the world tune in to his show, ready to follow him on an underwater adventure with a side of erotic fantasy.

Not me. I'd been fooled once.

At the last minute, my guardian angel had saved me from catching myself on that line. So instead of being one of the long string of women he nibbled on and set aside, I was churned-up chum in the wake of Hurricane Anton. One of those thrown back for whom the erotic stayed a fantasy.

I'd extracted myself as quickly as I could, ditching France for the Seychelles at the first opportunity. Hiding out on a tropical paradise outside the cyclone belt, where I'd be safe.

Yet, here came Hurricane Anton whirling into my hotel, sexy, tanned, on a new adventure, broadcasting that devastating smile every one of his million viewers felt was only for them.

"*Bonzour.*" Nic waved and greeted them in Kreol, the local language I was still learning. "Welcome to Makarios."

"Which is currently not open." I glared at Anton, determined not to notice how even the environment conspired to showcase his beauty: the island breeze ruffled his thick hair, and the apricot midmorning light bronzed his muscled skin. He looked like a god risen from the sea, and I knew damn well the gods played games with humans.

"Saba Sweet," he said in that delicious accent, French flavored with Morocco. He remembered my name. "*La belle* Saba."

"Still not open." I looked pointedly at his bag. "Who sent you here?"

"Bernard."

I held back a groan. My manager. "No, no, no."

He flashed those white teeth, one charmingly crooked. "Yes, yes, yes."

The chant was too close to what I imagined his women called out in the midst of the one night they were allotted. I scowled at him as I grabbed my phone and checked the signal. Not great, but not absent, which could sometimes happen on Mahé. I tapped out a text.

Nic drew me aside. "Okay, clearly the dive boy wants you." She held up a hand to cover her stage whisper. "Do I have a shot with Curly?"

"That's Bougie." I shielded my face with my phone and tried not to look at any of them. Beaujean, Anton's best friend and right-hand man, went everywhere with him. "You can have him if you don't mind the mileage."

Bougie got almost as much action as Anton did. Actually, more, as he cleaned up Anton's leftovers and the rejects. Bougie hadn't made a play for me, but then again, I'd cleared out fast to leave the dust of humiliation behind me.

Until it caught up with me.

At my hotel.

"Boo-jee." Nic gave a low whistle. "Hope his mama don't ever know what I plan to do to him."

"Nic, they're not staying."

"*Tifi*, Chief Dive Boy will go wherever you put him. You see the looks he giving you? Tuck that man in your bed right now and give him a kiss for later."

"That didn't work the first time." I turned away when her eyes flared and she grabbed my arm.

"I want that story."

"So," Anton called. "Saba. You're running this place now?" He drummed his palms on my desk, tapping to a rhythm in his head.

The man lived to music, either humming, joining his deep voice in harmony with a song, or swinging along to his own relaxed beat. Many times, I'd walked down to the beach in Hyères to find Anton, up to his knees in cobalt blue water, holding some fantastic sea animal for the camera close-up.

I'd seen those long, brown fingers wrapped around a tall cool glass in the shade of a cabana, and once around the neck of a sweating beer when I'd ventured out to a local club with the guys.

More than once, I'd seen those well-shaped, clever hands brush the shoulder or back of a woman who looked like she'd recently stepped away from a Saint Laurent photo shoot. A woman who appeared once or twice at dinner, came to watch an hour or so of shooting, then drifted away with the tide, making way for the next day's catch.

I looked away from his criminally beautiful face, and out of habit, scanned the empty lanai for anything out of place. A few of Anton's team had settled into the bamboo and palm fiber furniture, trading banter. I didn't have the heart to tell them to get up. My design was working just as I'd planned it to, inviting guests to linger, creating spaces for people to connect.

"I'm overseeing the reopening of Makarios," I told Anton. "Bernard made some major renovations when he bought the place. He hopes to relaunch shortly after Christmas, and I'm here to make that happen."

After embarrassing myself in France, I'd taken the most distant location I could find. A remote island country in the Indian Ocean, a thousand miles from anywhere, sounded like exactly the place I could hide until my wounded pride recovered.

Yet here stood the man I'd been trying to escape. The universe certainly had a sense of humor.

"You have an interesting job," Anton said. That steel-blue gaze made my skin prickle. "Running all over the world, turning around luxury hotels and resorts."

I bit my lip. Praise? From Anton? I was pretty sure he thought I was an idiot. So said the look on his face when I made my one drunken and highly regretted pass at him.

"Some would say you have the best job," I said. "Filming underwater treasures. Teaching people about the fantastic creations that live beneath the surface of the sea."

He nodded. His hair, closely cropped when we first met, curled into soft black waves that begged for a woman to slide her hands in and to scrape her fingers against his scalp.

Nope, not my hands.

"And I also survey marine health for governments." His plush, perfect lips were moving. I shook off the buzz of attraction and tried to keep up. "The Seselwa ministry hired us to do a study on the Port Launay Marine Park, report on the populations and such. Bernard asked us to look at a couple of his projects while we're here."

He said Seselwa, the Kreol name for the country, moving as easily between French, English, and Kreol as natives like Nic did.

Anton fit in anywhere, as adaptable as the sea creatures he studied. He could camouflage better than a shark.

"You know Bernard?" The way the surprises were coming at me today, my mother would hop off a helicopter with her luggage, and it would snow for Christmas.

Anton shrugged, and I stared at the sleek line of his clavicle, the cap of muscle on his arm. Every part of this man was a masterpiece. I'd held out as long as I could in France, but it was no wonder I'd succumbed to the seductive charge. He simply had to stand in front of a woman and she'd melt.

I waved the small fan I'd bought on my first visit to Victoria, the capital city. The humidity on Mahé couldn't match my hometown's, but it'd been ten years since I lived in Mississippi.

"Where did Bernard say you would stay? The rooms aren't ready."

He grinned, those plummy lips parting over that one leaning tooth. "What about yours?"

The nerve of him, to tease me after he'd turned me down in the south of France. I hadn't thought he was cruel.

I gulped, mentally flailing.

I couldn't do this. Have him stay at my hotel.

He had to go.

A shout from the guys made me drop my fan. Within the garden enclosure, which ran alongside the lanai, a huge, rounded shape heaved itself onto four legs and waddled out from the dense shadow of a tropical tree. A leathery gray snout emerged into the sunlight, followed by a pair of black, blinking eyes. Then the enormous creature shuffled toward the fence.

"No way." Anton's face broke into that delighted, kid-in-a-candy-store expression that his viewers waited for week after week. "You have a giant tortoise."

His delight breached my barriers. The huge, adorable animal broke the tension, as they do. "That's Zippy coming to say hi. Wanna give her a treat?"

"Absolutely."

Zippy clomped toward us on her stubby legs, hauling her massive domed shell along. She'd been fascinated by the glittering Christmas tree I'd set up by the reception desk, and came regularly to inspect it, stretching her ropy neck toward the plastic branches.

Anton touched my fingers when I held out the carrot I carried in my bag. His skin slid over mine like beach sand, silky and rough at the same time.

He approached Zippy, carrot extended, and whooped with joy when she sniffed, nibbled, then yanked the treat from his hand. His eyes shone with delight when he turned to me, and my insides swirled like waves hitting a beach.

"You," he said, "have made my day. And also—is that a jellyfish tree?"

I nodded, mirroring his grin. "There are a couple on the grounds, and we have a bunch of young seedlings in the greenhouse."

"Those trees don't exist anywhere else in the world. That—" he pointed at Zippy— "you can't find anywhere else in the world. This place is amazing." He turned in a circle, taking in the lanai, his scattered friends, the tended grounds of the resort, the winding paths leading to the villas, the thicket of palm forest greening the slopes of Morne Seychellois, and the giant of a mountain dozing in the background. "I couldn't wait to get back here."

"You've been to the Seychelles before?" He'd never mentioned it. Not that I'd noted every word he said, on camera or elsewhere.

"Bougie and I came here five years ago to help set up Port

Launay. Did a lot of the initial observation and reports." A bird call split the air, and he looked around for the source. A small gray bird perched on the hibiscus, the iridescent green patch at his throat jerking as he spat a series of high, harsh notes.

"Sunbird," Anton said in wonder.

"*Kolibri*," I said, showing off one of the Kreol words I'd learned. I'd fallen under the spell with him. "There's so much on these islands that is rare and beautiful. I am absolutely in love with this place."

The beaches were a postcard of paradise, the classic image of glistening white sand shaded with palms and horizons cradling satiny blue water. But there was so much more. Palm forests carpeted high hills, and huge granite boulders scattered the seashore like pebbles left by a giant's game. The winds played their gentle music from the northwest for half the year, southeast the rest.

Anton faced me, his steel-blue eyes scorching. We stood there as if we were the only two people in the world.

"Saba Sweet," he said, and his voice was low, nothing like the chatty tone he used in his videos. "In love in the Seychelles."

I narrowed my eyes. There was a taunt in there somewhere, of that I was sure. For weeks, we'd mingled in the south of France, his crew staying at my hotel while they filmed, but we'd never gotten to know one another. I knew the Anton Olivier who grinned and gestured for the camera, who flirted with women and joked with the guys. But the sharp mind moving behind those glittering eyes was a mystery to me.

"Not in love." I scowled. "Not with anyone."

He did a head-to-toe sweep, tracking my black kinky hair caught back with a twisted scarf as a headband. He had to notice my latte skin had turned browner in the tropical sun. I curled my fingers to hide my chipped nail polish since I never seemed to have the time for a manicure.

His smoldering gaze trailed heat everywhere it moved. "Maybe you should fix that," he whispered.

I dropped my gaze, certain now he was taunting me, which was outrageous given he'd been the one to reject my advances. The arrogance. "Don't get... Damn it." I growled as a text came through. "Bernard says you get the Villa Royale. It's ready, and it should fit all of you."

He flashed his cocky grin. "Yes. Unless..." He lifted a thick black brow. "You're inviting me to share your room?"

"No." I waved my fan wildly.

His grin turned wicked and sensual. "Okay, not yet. But we're on an island, *La Belle* Saba. You can't run away from me again."

***

That afternoon I walked one of the small paths of Makarios to the spa area, winding through the humid emerald shade beneath thief palm and pandan, the leaves of which, one of our herbalists told me, they used in the spa treatment, though I couldn't imagine to what purpose. I didn't have time for spa treatments. There was still too much to do to get the resort ready.

I spotted a few Indian mulberry shrubs among the casuarina and made a note to tell Bernard. He didn't like the fruit, which, when ripe, smelled like rancid cheese. But this plant also had many medicinal properties, and the herbalist had prescribed a daily glass of Indian mulberry juice to my diet the day after I arrived.

"Keep skin fresh," Lanying had said, patting my cheek. "Keep you young." I didn't doubt I'd looked worn when I arrived. Tired and dehydrated from alcohol, and copious tears of shame.

Clustered around the main pavilion, the red bead trees threw their arms out in welcome. Lanying had explained the properties of this plant as well, notably that the bright red seeds, shaped like hearts, were called the love bean in China, and were made into jewelry or exchanged as tokens of mutual love. The thought, then as now, made my skin flush with thoughts of Anton.

Mutual love. I couldn't say I'd ever known that.

I'd known infatuation. Convenience. Passion, now and again.

Why did Anton Olivier show up at my hotel, uninvited, unannounced, and now I was thinking about love beans?

The long, low room with the exercise pool was unlocked and empty. "Hello?" My voice echoed in the wood-lined space. Most of the staff had left for the holidays, but a maintenance worker was supposed to meet me. "Someone said there's a problem with the pool?"

The turquoise blue water in the long spa churned with activity. The exercise pool was one of Bernard's fancier additions, with its hydromassage jets, adjustable current, temperature control, and built-in exercise equipment. But the belt of the treadmill rattled along the bottom, and the arms of the rowing bars circled faster than any human could keep up.

A low growl from the overworked equipment filled the room as I walked along the wall, tugging on one decorative copalwood square after another until I found the control panel. The main switch quieted the treadmill, but not the whirring of the rowing machine, still twirling like the antennae of a deranged oversized insect.

Great. Now what? I didn't particularly want to get my Reiss linen jumpsuit wet. The Emilia was one of my favorite outfits. The V neck outlined my breasts without making my cleavage look obscene, and the high waist gave my legs a nice long silhouette. It was helped by the flirty drape of extra fabric at the waist, a long dagger that made more slimming vertical lines.

I tapped a few texts, but wasn't surprised when no answering dots danced back. One of the selling points of the spa was no cell reception, and no WiFi. Guests had to leave the rest of the world behind.

Super. This was one of those times when maintenance technician fell under my job description. Saba Sweet, head gal, complaint manager, and all-around fixer.

Too bad the problem wasn't timing how long it would take a server to walk from the juice bar to deliver a nice cool SeyBrew beer to that relaxing palmwood chaise draped with cushions. I'd been hoping for an easy solution today, especially with Hurricane Anton blowing into my quiet refuge.

I laid my cell phone in my hemp sandals and stretched out beside the pool, the natural stone cool and hard against my breasts and hips. Warm water swirled around my arm as I probed the inside wall of the pool for the control buttons. Pressing them did nothing. I wiggled forward to extend my reach and that's when it happened: the flirty flare of fabric at the waist of my lovely jumpsuit fell into the water, wrapped instantly around the churning rowing handle, and jerked me into the pool headfirst.

I surfaced, sputtering, clinging to the handle as it maniacally beat the water. I was going to drown here in the Seychelles without getting to say good-bye to my mother. Losing me, her only child, would kill her. And I'd die without achieving any of the things I'd imagined I'd have someday: a husband, kids, a house, and maybe a hotel of my own. I was strapped tight to the mechanism, and even as I wriggled and pushed, I knew I was trapped in wet linen, swaddled as tight as a baby on its mother's chest.

"Hello," I yelled into the nothingness of the empty room, hoping my voice would carry into the equally empty spa village beyond with small thatched patios offering individual treatment rooms quietly awaiting guests. If I drowned here, I'd never get to walk the Kniepp footbath with its textured path.

A Seychelles warbler chirped at me. Bernard would be happy we had warblers. A little tree frog regarded me through the window from his perch on a fern.

"Don't just sit there," I snapped at him, clinging to the whizzing handle for dear life. "Get help."

He stared back with his bulbous eyes, unperturbed by my predicament.

I wiggled my shoulders. I could try to tear myself free, but the wet fabric had no give. There was a reason the Egyptians wrapped mummies in linen, which survived for thousands of years.

A vise clenched my waist, the fabric wrapped hard around one of the handles. I couldn't shimmy my hips through that small opening even if I managed to wriggle out of my straps. Whatever I did, I was going to ruin this three-hundred-dollar jumpsuit. Then, if I did manage to climb out of my clothing, for sure someone would see me wet and naked before I could make it back to my room.

Hard enough to be taken seriously as a young woman in designer wear. If I showed up wrapped in a spa towel because I'd gotten stuck in the exercise pool, I'd lose every ounce of respect I'd won from the staff.

Did I want to drown or did I want to be alive and naked? I struggled harder, clinging to the rotating handle with one arm to hold myself above water while using my free arm to tug at my shoulder strap.

I'd managed to get one of the spaghetti straps to my elbow and was about to bare my breasts to all of Makarios when I heard a wonderful sound above the chirp of frogs and insects and warblers: human voices coming from somewhere on the path.

"Hello. Need a little help here," I shrieked with desperation. I couldn't let them walk by. I clung to the whizzing row bar with both arms, hoping I'd be heard above the growl of machinery. "In here. Help!"

Three people stepped onto the porch: Bernard, Lanying, and Anton.

Lanying slapped her hands to her face and cried out. Bernard uttered some expression in Kreol—I was pretty sure it was a curse I'd heard Nic use—then sped across the room to the far wall.

Anton didn't hesitate. He dove into the pool, a clean, efficient, professional dive, and in under a second he was beside me, all shimmery mahogany skin, wet black hair, and searing silver-blue eyes.

"Don't panic," he said in French.

"I'm panicking." My voice sounded weak, but not from fighting the machine. I'd lost my breath. Anton Olivier this close to me made my head go light and empty, like a luscious, exotic scent that overpowered all the other senses.

He wrapped one arm around me, and that was another shock—Anton Olivier's arm around me. With his free hand he groped along my waist, following the path of the fabric sucked into the pocket where the rowing arm still churned, destroying my favorite and most flattering outfit.

"I'm stuck," I said.

"I've got you."

Bernard opened a fuse box I hadn't seen and threw a switch. The whirling antennae of the rowing machine powered down. Anton's words hung in the sudden silence.

Bernard sputtered in Kreol, pushing his gold-rimmed glasses back up his nose. "Knew that guy didn't know what he was doing," he fumed. "Knew there would be problem. Saba, *koma sava? Blese?*"

"I'm not hurt." But I felt woozy, my body surging with adrenaline and relief, and having Anton Olivier so close to me.

He used both hands to unwrap my clothing from the machinery, his movements deft and delicate. The lightheaded feeling floated all through me, as if I were very, very drunk.

"Short in the wiring?" Anton asked, setting me free.

Bernard shook his head. "Mon'n calling him Lendi. He fix this."

"I'm sure it can wait until after Christmas." My voice wobbled.

I found my feet and stepped away from Anton, letting the water separate us. It caressed the top of his deliciously carved pecs. The man had a painfully perfect physique.

Though the water was a comfortable temperature, I started to shiver.

Bernard frowned. "You could have been hurt."

"I'm okay, Bernard. Alarmed, yes. And embarrassed."

I headed toward the ladder, aware that Anton was right behind me, as if to keep anything from seizing me again.

I climbed out of the pool, arms and legs shaking from adrenaline, aware that my ass was essentially in Anton's face. I dripped on the pool deck, the wet linen of my jumpsuit molded like papier-mâché to my body, outlining every curve and dimple.

Anton surfaced like a young sea god and shook water from his hair like a puppy.

Then his gaze fell on my neckline, gaping open with one strap draped down my arm, the fabric skimming my rock-hard nipple.

He froze as if the row bar had whacked him on the head. Hastily I shoved the strap back onto my shoulder, and Anton looked away.

"Aiyah," Lanying cried. "You are soaked through. You need to change into dry things and drink hot tea." She rushed over with an enormous Egyptian cotton spa towel that smelled like orange and jasmine, and she wrapped it around me, rubbing my arms with vigor.

I lowered my head while she patted my thick hair.

I'd been plotting how to appear sophisticated, elegant, and carefree like the kind of effortlessly glamorous woman Anton dated in France. I'd meant to show him what he'd missed when he turned me down.

Now he'd had to rescue me, like a helpless nitwit, and I was sunk forever into the *not my type* category. No wonder he wouldn't look at me.

He cleared his throat and addressed Bernard. "There was, uh, that thing you wanted to show me?"

Bernard's face cleared. "*Wi*. And now Saba is here, she can tell us—"

"Saba is going straight to her villa to change," Lanying scolded. "And put ginger in her tea, and maybe turmeric."

Bernard rubbed a hand across his bald head. "Okay, *byen*. But, Saba, can you serve dinner at Helios tonight?"

I swallowed an automatic protest. All the resort restaurants were closed for the holiday except for the casual cabana, which we kept open for us. With our chef away, the staff would need help feeding a crowd of burly men.

As much as I wanted to, I couldn't hide from Anton. I had to make his crew comfortable. He was our guest.

I snuck a peek at him. He was dripping and unconcerned by the T-shirt and shorts plastered to his skin. And why wouldn't he be completely at ease in that body? Lean, muscled, a perfect body that I'd spent way too much time imagining since I left France. That body dancing, diving, kicking a ball on the beach, or draped in a lounge chair. And in my imagination, because it was fantasy and I could do whatever I wanted, the woman beside that splendid body, gazing into that strikingly beautiful face, was me.

Well, I'd had my chance, and I'd blown it. Twice.

"Sure," I croaked. "I'll see to dinner."

Bernard and Anton left, and I hid my face in the towel with a groan.

Clearly, I hadn't run far enough.

***

"Tell me what happened between you two."

Nic walked with me through the updated kitchen of Helios, overseeing preparations for dinner.

The pastry chef was in Mauritius, and the head chef had gone home to Kenya, but the sous chef had no problem whipping up a meal for a dozen hungry men.

Trevally simmered in coconut milk, heart of palm steeped in lemon water for a salad, and meat I suspected was fruit bat steeped in a vinegar marinade, ready to fold into a spicy curry.

I hadn't been brave enough to try that local delicacy, but fruit bat curry kept down the population of flying foxes that emerged each evening and made a huge racket among the papaya and passion fruit trees.

A pile of bananas sat next to a bottle of *buka,* the local rum made with sugarcane. Nic poured us each a glass of *kalou,* palm wine.

I sipped with caution. I was here to ensure dinner moved smoothly from the remodeled kitchen to the refurbished dining room, and that all my new touches worked as planned. I didn't intend to linger.

"Nothing happened between us." I sipped my wine, hoping to signal the conversation was over.

"That's definitely not the case." She swirled a glass in the air, indicating the group of men lounging in the dining area.

They'd donned shirts and sandals in a nod to the dress code, but bantered as boisterously as ever.

Bougie glanced our way every so often, as if keeping an eye on us—or Nic—but Anton didn't turn around. Sunglasses perched on his head, dive watch strapped to his wrist, Teva sandals on his feet, and his linen shirt several buttons undone, he made casual chic look casually sexy.

I was *not* falling for it again.

"There is some vibe between you," Nic said. "Even I can see it."

I sighed and braced myself with another long sip. "You want to know what happened? We went dancing one night, I drank too much, I made a pass at him. He was appalled. I was humiliated. I left. He's here."

Nic blinked. "He turned you down? *You*?"

"The guy dates international models and Olympic athletes, Nic. I'm hardly in that league."

I nodded and smiled at a prep cook, a local and a student in the hospitality program at the University of Seychelles. He'd move up to line cook once he graduated, if I had my say.

Though I might not. I would be here only a couple of months, and then I'd move on.

My job as consultant meant I was the person who'd been brought in to lift up, turn around, and redesign the hotel. Then I trained up other people and turned the hotel over to them. I'd redone a dozen major luxury hotels and resorts, and I had no place that was truly mine.

Nic tapped her chin and looked me over. My jumpsuit was drying on the line back at my villa. I'd traded it for a wraparound dress that allowed ease of movement, and my comfy Dulcie London sandals, since tonight I meant to walk through the new family village and make sure the poolside rooms were finished. Then I'd buckle down with the books.

I wasn't here to drift among the cloud of testosterone trying to entice men, though I could probably find that sort of entertainment for the night if I wanted.

There was no formal policy, but guys with wives and girlfriends didn't tend to stick with Anton's footloose crew, or at least didn't bring their partners to projects.

Problem was, I didn't handle one-night stands well, and Anton Olivier's relationships fell into the blink-and-you'll-miss-it category.

"You are your own league, Saba. *Tifi*, look at you." Nic held out my free arm and gave me a top-to-toe survey.

I didn't see what she saw. I saw too much hair and too much roundness. In a few months, I'd be thirty. No more excuses for reckless behavior.

When my mother turned thirty, I'd been six. She'd gone back to work full time, and her husband got tenure. All I had on my list of accomplishments was a full-time job.

I glanced through the open kitchen to the dining area where the guys sat near the channel of water that ferried the occasional leaf or water bug around the edge of the seating area.

Anton watched us. Even across the room, his stare grazed my skin like a touch.

I had to show him I wasn't some silly, helpless dimwit who needed rescuing. I was a woman with class and talent, and he'd blown his chance.

Actually, I had to pour my class and talent into my job and make Makarios ready for opening. "Let's focus here, Nic. I've got a lot to get done before Christmas."

With guests here, we'd need staff to work the holiday. I'd planned a holiday party for my crew, a thank you for all their hard work, and I meant for that to happen no matter what guests were getting in the way.

I pulled out a tray woven of palm fiber and piled it with appetizers: fish balls, chilli cakes, and chickpeas spiced with cumin and ginger. I popped a plantain chip in my mouth, then sent the boat floating down the channel to our guests.

Floating dinners were a big hit at other island resorts, and I grinned when I heard the exclamations of delight as the guys captured the basket and began to demolish the delicacies. I walked over with a tray of drinks.

"Palm wine?" Anton's low rasp sounded like he'd spent a long day chatting to the camera. I couldn't brace myself for the blueness of those eyes.

"Tapped right up the mountain." I held the tray toward him. "We try to source as much locally as we can."

"This place is amazing, Saba." Bougie leaned over and grabbed a glass, cheerfully jostling his boss. "I plan to live in the Royale forever, by the way. Never leaving. I'll earn my keep."

"Great, we need housekeepers," I said. "Bernard must really like you, giving you the Villa Royale. That's our presidential suite."

"I've heard the honeymoon suite is the best." Anton watched me over his glass.

"Half our rooms are honeymoon suites." I tried to sound lighthearted and carefree. "Honeymooners are big business in the Seychelles."

"Sit down." Bougie kicked Ferhad's feet off the chair next to Anton and brushed the cushion with his hand. Then he cleared a seat next to him. "Your friend too. Tell us what you've been doing since France."

"I'd love to, but dinner—"

"Join us." Anton reached out for my hand but drew back as if he'd reconsidered, though not before his fingers brushed my wrist. "We want to hear." Heat raced up my arm.

In the pool, he'd touched me because he had to. This gesture looked like he couldn't help himself. My blood pounded in my veins as my body sank into the chair.

"I've been here, working at Makarios." I was amazed I was able to speak. "What about you?"

Anton's face lit up, his rapt expression endearing. "We did a show on the marine park at Alonissos and dived the Peristera shipwreck. It's this ancient Athenian boat. Amazing. One of the best underwater walls I've seen, and they put in these live cameras with continuous feeds. They're talking about expanding the dive tours to other shipwrecks, so we did some trial runs. And then Bernard called."

"But it's Christmas." We moved to a long table and the prep cook wheeled out the meal, platter after steaming platter in brightly colored ceramic dishes. "Didn't you guys want to be home with your families?"

"I'll see my family," Nic said, diving into the trevally. "Seychellois have big parties. My family lays a buffet on the beach and we eat all day. Starts right after Christmas mass. You all should come."

Bougie nodded. "Maybe I will. Detroit was too far away to get a decent flight. I'll go visit the fam once we're done here. Boss promised me a nice bonus, and I haven't seen my nieces and nephews in months."

It'd been nearly a year since I saw my mother. My heart pinched. It wasn't Christmas without my mom's cinnamon candles, mulled wine, and a thoughtful gift she'd made herself, then wrapped in handmade paper.

"What about you?" I asked, turning to Anton.

He lifted his shoulders, let them fall. "My parents decided to go to Iceland for the holiday. They invited me and my sister, but she's in Ecuador on some trip for Doctors Without Borders. I might stop by Morocco when we're done. My mom's parents are getting older and they don't like to travel anymore."

I'd learned from comments on his show, and through off hours, that Anton's father was a museum director in Paris and his mother was born in Tangier. They'd met when she came to study cooking at

Le Cordon Bleu. Anton had grown up primarily in France but traveled widely as a kid. He was a citizen of the world, educated, cosmopolitan, and in a league way above most guys I knew.

If I didn't wrap this evening up soon, I was going to be foolish and throw myself at him again.

"What about your family, Saba?" Nic asked.

I hadn't told her much about my past. I made it a personal policy not to open up too much at my locations. Not to get too invested.

I looked at Nic so I didn't have to face Anton. "I'm an only kid, and my mom and I don't really do Christmas anymore. My dad died five years ago, around Thanksgiving, and that Christmas…we didn't feel much like celebrating." Or any Christmas since, as it had turned out. "She's actually at an ashram in India right now. She's been there for a while."

Long enough to meet somebody she'd fallen in love with. She hadn't dated since Dad died, hadn't even talked about other men, and now she was in love. I was still trying to come to grips with that.

"I might visit her once I've got things set up here," I went on, since everybody was staring at me as if I'd grown another head. I should've known better than to bring up my dad. Talking about him ripped the scab off a wound that hadn't healed yet, and I was sure my grief showed on my face. "I've never been to India."

"Where'd you grow up?" Anton asked, his voice soft, his molten gaze fixed on me.

"Um, isn't it time for someone else's story?"

"Nope, still yours," Nic prompted.

Anton refilled my glass of palm wine. The liquid fizzed over my tongue, sweet and tart at the same time. Much like straying away from my responsibilities to linger here with Anton, drinking in his heady presence, knowing I'd feel aftereffects later.

"I grew up in the States, in Mississippi," I said. "My mom was born there, and so was I. My dad was from Cameroon. Yaoundé. He came to teach French and African studies at the University of Mississippi where my mom was studying to be a nurse. They married as soon as she graduated."

"So how did you get into the hospitality industry?" Anton again. This was more than we'd talked the entire time we'd been together in France.

I swirled my wine. The pond shimmered in its concrete channels, catching the setting sun in ripples of orange and gold. Above the tree canopy a blue pigeon courted his mate, plunging in a steep dive with his crown a blaze of red.

The air in Seychelles was a silk cloak all the time, like the finest and lightest of shawls.

I tugged my legs beneath me, leaned back in the chair. "My father worked hard, my mother harder, but they liked to save up to take one big vacation a year."

I smiled at the memories. "One year we camped. A couple of years, we backpacked. One year, thanks to a friend of my dad's, we went on a private African safari.

"But my mom liked the expensive hotels and resorts where she could have everything done for her. It always seemed to be a kind of magic, how everything got done so smoothly and you never saw how. It made her so relaxed. Refreshed her for what she had to deal with every other week, the sick patients, the worried families, me."

Bougie passed around the plate of plantain chips. "So you decided that's what you wanted to do?" Anton asked, taking a handful and passing the plate to me.

I crunched a chip. "My first real job was reception at a local hotel in Oxford, called the Graduate. It's only a four-star, but to me it was posh.

"They expanded into rentals, so I moved to that side for a while, and then I was in this ambassador program for them during college and traveled all over the States. After I graduated they sent me to the hotel in New York City, and then to the UK, and then I got invited to help out with a new boutique chain, and…" I turned up a hand with a shrug. "Things kept opening up after that. I got lucky, I guess."

"Or you're really, really good at what you do." Bougie winked.

Anton watched me. "You don't mind moving around so much?"

"I like seeing new places. Meeting new people." I nodded toward Nic.

"Hard to have a family, though," Nic said.

A pigeon coo floated on the breeze, followed by a soft response. The high flyer had apparently impressed his lady. I looked into my glass, dangerously empty.

"I haven't thought much about the future," I said.

I went through men like I went through contracts, with a new sweetheart in every port. I didn't plan it that way, but my relationships didn't seem to stick. The college boyfriend, the boyfriends after, the guy in Japan I was engaged to for a time, all those romances ran their course. The lease expired, and I moved on.

I stood. "Who wants dessert?"

"Ralph's bringing it." Nic waved her hand. "Anton, what got you started on your gig?"

"Ah." He leaned back, and his smile rooted me in place. I wanted to bask in it like a fresh rising sun.

"My father liked to dive in his spare time. The Green Bay caves in Cyprus. Portofino, Italy. When I was ten, he took me to Chios, in Greece, and I was hooked. I got my first job leading dives around Belle-Île-en-Mer, that's an island in Brittany, and then someone put an underwater camera in my hands—"

"And I taught him how to use it," Bougie said. "And now he's Anton Olivier, showing you the wonders beneath the waves."

"To waves." Nic raised her glass. We drank. "I bet you move around too much to keep a relationship going," she said. "Kind of like Saba."

I glared, trying to ward off her obvious hints. The fruit bats finished their noisy evening feast and congregated in the flame tree, their bodies dark clumps against the brilliant red.

I went to the bar and turned on the lights, which hung in paper lanterns and fabric cages crafted by local artists. The gleam of the wooden tabletops and mellow glow of the water cast the relaxed, intimate feel I wanted.

One success, at least.

"I never got why you two didn't hook up in France." Bougie popped the last chilli cake into his mouth and licked his fingers. "I mean, everyone else made a play for Saba. Got turned down, though."

"She froze 'em out?" Nic guessed.

"Tromped us flat, that's what," Bougie confirmed. He sliced his hand through the air. "So we all wondered why Anton didn't make a move."

"Didn't want to be tromped," Anton said "My ego couldn't handle it."

Ferhad, one of the sound techs, laughed. "We figured, since she shut down all of us, she was holding out for you."

I glared at Ferhad. We'd chatted once about the earthquake damage in İskenderun, where he was from, and nothing about our conversation had carried a hint of flirtation.

"Why should I be the one to get lucky?" Anton asked, avoiding the scowl I turned on him.

"Uh, cuz you're the face?" Bougie circled a hand before his own visage. "I mean, we make you look good, but the dames go for you. Every time."

"And then they learn what a disappointment I am." Anton refilled his wine.

"Disappointment?" Disbelief resounded in the word hurtling out of me before I could catch it.

He poured carefully, as if judging how drunk he dared get. "You've noticed they don't stick around, right?" He added another pour.

Bougie spoke for me. "Cuz they have an expiration date," he said.

Anton shook his head. "Because they're disappointed. They think they're getting caviar and champagne, and a cameo on the show. Then they find out I'd rather have a beer on the beach at sunset with merguez and falafel. Maybe truffle fries if I want to live wild."

I loved merguez, a Moroccan sausage. I'd eaten it on a baguette with mustard and as much cumin as I could stand at least once a week while in Paris.

My mouth watered at the memory even as Anton's admission twisted in my chest. No one could be disappointed in him. He was the amazing Anton Olivier.

"I get it," Bougie said. "And Saba is a five-star-accommodations kind of girl."

"Way too good for me." Anton tipped back his wine.

"Can we move on from the topic of my dating life?" I said, my voice not quite steady. "Dessert's here."

Ralph, our hospitality student, pushed up the rolling cart. Bananas swam on brightly flowered plates, puddled in a caramel sauce spiced with rum. I switched off the lights and Ralph lit the rum, searing small fires to life all over the cart.

Light danced in Anton's eyes, burnishing his skin, and my mouth went dry.

"*Bannen flamben.*" Ralph beamed and we all clapped, praising him for his performance and our sous chef for the magnificent meal.

We tucked into the treat, and I allowed myself an expansive look around the table.

Maybe I was hazy with palm wine and rum.

Maybe I was giddy from Anton's nearness.

But in that moment, this restaurant on the fringe of Mahé, empty but for us, felt like the center of the world, and the most beautiful place I'd ever been.

"So Bernard said you'd come with us tomorrow while I look at the desalination pipes." Anton addressed me.

I tamped down the insane urge to lean over and lick the gleam of rum from his lips.

"Um… He did?" I didn't know anything about the desalination setup.

"You're dive certified, right?"

"For open water," I said cautiously.

Passing my training dive and getting my first-level PADI certification for scuba had been the reason his crew took me out dancing at the cabana on the beach. I'd wanted to learn to dive, and the south of France seemed the place.

That was the night when I drank too much, got brave dreams, and asked Anton if he wanted to walk me to my room.

Big mistake.

"I need to check the intake pipes, and you have the blueprints. You can point me to the right place." I opened my mouth to tell him anyone could read blueprints, but he went on to say, "Bring a swimsuit, water, and lots of sunscreen. We'll meet on the beach at oh six hundred."

"You need six hundred people to check the desalination pipes?"

"That's fancy talk for six o'clock," Bougie said. "See you there, Saba."

I thought of a dozen reasons I was a rotten candidate for this job.

Why would Bernard even suggest it? My strengths were hospitality, not mechanical or infrastructure.

But this would be my first real dive. With Anton Olivier, an absolute pro. Who made my heart race in a way it hadn't since I couldn't remember when.

He was dangerous to my senses, and he made me want things I knew I couldn't have.

I'd be a dope to spend more time with him, soak in his energy and passion, get scorched by his charisma.

I *was* a dope, because I was going.

I scraped the last of the rum-soaked caramel from my plate and caught Anton watching as I licked my spoon. His gaze tracked the utensil, my tongue, and my mouth.

A fire lit deep inside me as I rubbed my lips together and he watched that too.

Something was happening here.

His cell phone rang a bright calypso tune.

Anton's expression as he read the display looked like Christmas had come early. He soared out of his chair and trotted away, switching to French. "Finally. Where have you been?" His voice poured warm delight.

"Must be Marina, the Moldovan model," Bougie said with a grunt, taking Anton's glass of wine.

"Or Ula, the Finnish graduate student," Ferhad said. "What was she studying again?"

"Anton." Bougie drained Anton's glass.

I stood and cleared the plates.

Their banter affirmed what I'd already known. I had no business letting my heart patter or do anything else around Anton Olivier.

***

It wasn't a lie to say the Seychelles breeze caressed the skin like a lover. Near the water a breeze always tumbled, brisk enough to blow clouds away, or gentle enough to soothe the tropical heat.

Palm fronds dipped and swayed to a natural music, and a hunting kestrel loosed its high, wild cry. All of it called up some wildness in me.

Morning sunlight blushed the white sand rose, and the blue sky deepened near the edges of land and sea, warmed by the contact.

I carried my shoes, catching the hum of the island's life through my bare feet. I hadn't been joking when I told Anton I was in love with the Seychelles. The islands had cast their spell over me.

He stood ankle-deep in the water, half-zipped into his shortie wetsuit, black with red lines tracing the contours of his body. His back was a wall of lean muscle, his biceps knotted as he held a pair of binoculars to his face.

I swallowed hard.

"The fairy terns are feeding their baby." He motioned me forward and held out the binoculars. "Look."

The strap hung around his neck, and I had to step close to lift the lenses, bringing my face mere inches from his.

His shoulder brushed mine as he pointed. "There, in the takamaka tree."

I followed his fingers through the binoculars and saw them, the mother a pink outline in the pearled light, the father dipping in with a fish flashing silver from his beak. A puffy fledgling rocked on the branch, cautious, then pecked at his breakfast.

"Sweet little family." Anton's voice rumbled near my ear, then moved inside my chest.

I pushed the binoculars back at him, gasping for breath through the longing that pounded my chest like a breakwater wave.

Family, another thing I couldn't have. A guy had to stay to build a nest and raise a child.

"We ready to go?" My voice sounded uneven.

He pushed his arms into the suit and turned his back for me to zip. Oh God, I had to touch him.

I tugged up the zipper, trying, and failing, not to brush his skin. Firm, warm, gleaming bronze skin.

This was torture.

Bougie floated the boat close to shore. "Found it," he called.

Anton turned to me. "We have a shortie for you. Women's cut. Should fit." His gaze skimmed my body. I was tucked into a sensible, sturdy lapsuit giving me plenty of coverage: no side boob, no ass cheek. I'd thought about a flirty cut-out or my bikini, to see if I could make Anton's jaw drop, but that felt too obvious. This was a business trip.

Anton's breath changed and his look lingered a beat too long on my breasts.

He wheeled to Bougie, his voice rasping. "Hand it over."

I zipped myself into the clean black shortie. It sculpted my hips and boobs and pulled in my belly.

Anton tugged me into the boat. On shore he'd played it cool and easy, but his palm was sweaty.

I tucked away a grin.

"Good conditions out there," Bougie reported. "Clear for miles."

He handed Anton two sets of diving gear, already assembled. I wasn't surprised when Anton checked again, opening air valves and inspecting rings.

His gaze measured me, his eyes blue as a welding torch. My skin heated despite the breeze. I'd given up trying to tame my hair in this humidity, and my natural curls sprang everywhere.

The boat rocked, making me sway. "Need more weight for her belt," Anton said. "She'll be buoyant as hell."

"Excuse me," I said, not sure if that was an insult.

I'd passed my class and knew the steps, but nervous energy skimmed through me as Anton tightened my weight belt and lifted the BCD onto my shoulders, cinching buckles and straps. He breathed into my backup regulator, and it was as if he were breathing on my neck, a lover's caress.

Sun heated my skin.

He grabbed my hand. "This is how to release my weight belt." He pressed my palm against the catch at his waist, his body firm against my fingers. "And here's my inflator." He pushed my hand against his BCD, as solid as the muscle beneath. "Lean on me," he said as I struggled to put on my fins, his shoulder as firm and warm as the rest of him. I curled my fingers into the muscle and squeezed my toes in my fins.

"Remember the hand signals?" I nodded and repeated as he walked me through the signs for okay, up and down, something's wrong, and I need air. "Okay, buddy check," he said, preparing to turn, then stopped as he glimpsed my face.

"Saba." His voice was firm, professional. "You're my buddy, right? Do you trust me?"

I gulped and nodded. I trusted him with my life. But *his* life—I was responsible for him down there.

My first real dive, and Anton Olivier's life was in my charge.

He took my hands in his. Heat skipped up my arms, shimmery as the sun sailing above us. "Do you trust me?" he said again.

My gear dragged at my shoulders and back. Sweat squirmed

beneath my suit. The fins pinched my toes, and the mask pressed my head.

"Yes." I croaked out the words. "I trust you."

"Good. I trust you. Now check me." He turned his back and I patted over his gear with Bougie supervising. Anton pulled his mask into place and grinned at me, his face full of that fierce joy that lit the camera every time he was about to enter the water. "Follow me in."

He loved this. He sat on the edge of the boat, put in his regulator, and fell backward without a second of hesitation.

I glanced at Bougie, caught between panic and joy. Could I do this?

"You two will be a good team," Bougie said.

I sat on the edge of the boat, put in my regulator, and breathed the canned air. Sun baked my forehead. I had to calm down. I couldn't use up all my air. Anton had planned for two hours.

I would get to be with Anton, just us, in his world. I held one hand to my face, the other to my chest, and let myself fall.

He caught me with a hand on my back as I sank. I oriented myself, finding bottom and surface, stunned by the light slanting through the water. Anton was there, his hand on my wrist. His other hand circled finger to thumb. *Okay?*

I nodded, then remembered and signed back. *Okay.* I looked around and smiled against my regulator. I'd thought above ground was paradise. This was better. The world had gone blue as if we floated inside the sky.

Yet there was so much color. Knobs and shelves of coral, striped and speckled and lobed, mantled with sheets of fish in orange and yellow and silver.

Bushes of murky red strands floating and furling, conducting an orchestra of textures. Fans of bright fuchsia lace, discs of orange plating the rocks, clumps of dark green porcupine quills nodding.

A butterflyfish shot by, the white shell of its body lined with yellow fins, its orange beak poking my mask. I laughed, air burbling around my regulator, and the fish twisted away.

Anton wasn't taking in the scenery. He watched me. *Okay?* He signaled again.

I didn't know how to tell him this was better than okay. I wanted to stay here and never leave.

I held out my arms. *All this*, I tried saying. It was amazing.

He nodded, smiled, and took my hand.

That smile. It brought its own light.

And his hand on mine as we swam through this magical secret was nothing short of divine.

I'd looked at the blueprints last night, which were part of the design packet Bernard had sent me when I agreed to take this job. But I had no idea why he thought I needed to inspect the desalination system.

Anton knew what he was doing. We scalloped the shore until he found the pipe, the wire mesh screen clumped with seaweed. He replaced it with a different screen he extracted from a pouch hooked to his BCD.

I understood the concept: the goal was to take in water, but remove as little as possible of the microscopic life and larvae that would go on to become fish and food.

We floated a while longer, found a different pipe, the one that discharged any accidentally captured marine life back to the sea. Anton scraped away the seaweed there. He was zipping up his bag when I touched his arm and pointed.

A reef manta ray glided by us, a billowing skirt of white, the gills of his underside flaring. Anton watched it soar away, then turned, mirroring my grin.

He touched a finger to my cheek, pressing my dimple, and I reeled. I felt more connected to him through that single touch than I'd ever felt to another human being.

He tugged my hand, and I followed. Now it was time to play.

He had his watch and our navigator strapped to his wrist, so I went where he led.

We passed shelves of rock and boulders that bloomed like a rose garden, filled with red and pink and white. Coral cities belched life: blue angelfish veined with yellow, neon green wrasse splashed with red lava, soldierfish with their orange marble eyes and stern frowns.

A waterfall of fish veiled me when I drifted away, then suddenly Anton's hand parted the curtain, grasping my wrist. I startled, then looked where he pointed.

A hawksbill turtle paddled into view, light glinting off the dappled brown pattern of her shell and flippers, which camouflaged her among the rocks. A second turtle joined her. They looped through the water in their slow, acrobatic way, bouncing off one another's shells, poking each other with their beaky snouts. Buddies, or siblings. Or a mated pair. The beauty of them made my chest hurt.

Anton was watching me again. I patted a hand to my chest, telling him how beautiful I thought it was. He squeezed my wrist. Then he let go, and we swam on.

Time disappeared. The rest of the world ceased to exist. The universe held only us and each passing wonder.

My muscles started to ache and the water cooled as we swam deeper, but I didn't want to stop.

I knew better than to lose sight of Anton, but I lingered at one coral condominium, counting how many different types I could see: coral like brain lobes, coral like heart vessels, coral shaped like moon rocks, like mermaid hair, like fans.

I watched a hefty parrotfish, blushing green and purple, gnaw the coral and spit pebbles. I turned to tell Anton and came face-to-face with an enormous inhuman shape, a black eye the size of a saucer, dark speckling its bulging yellow body, its mouth big enough to swallow my skull.

Like an idiot, I screamed. My regulator popped from my mouth, and water rushed in. I flailed in panic, not knowing if I should scare the fish away or freeze.

I groped for my regulator, my backup, but my hands fisted water. Meanwhile the gargantuan thing that was about to eat me drifted closer, menacing, watching me choke.

Slight pressure at my back, a tug, and a regulator slid into my mouth. I sucked in air. Anton curled his arm around me, capturing my flailing hand.

The creature stared us down and bellied closer, mouth parting. Anton poked it—*poked* it—and the cavernous fish riffled and plowed away, keeping one glossy black eye turned toward us.

I hung sheltered in Anton's arms, my forehead on his shoulder as my breathing slowed and my heartbeat calmed. I realized the tube attached to my mouth led to his tank. He'd given me his backup regulator.

I was breathing his air.

He stroked my back in slow circles, as if soothing a child. Tiny electric shocks rose from the path his hand traced.

I groped for and found my own regulator, cleared it, traded his for mine. He passed his hand over my arms, as if checking. *Okay*?

I signaled back. *Okay*, because he had me.

Because nothing could hurt me while he was here.

He thumbed toward the surface. *Up*?

I agreed. He took my hand and we set out into the blue yonder. I didn't doubt he knew exactly where to go. I trusted him completely.

I'd never trusted anyone completely besides my parents. Then my dad died and left me, though not by choice, and now my mom had fallen in love again. She had dealt with her grief and was moving on, while I was simply moving on, trying to stay one step ahead of that gaping sense of loss.

Bougie waited at the pickup point. The boat didn't have a ladder, so Anton cupped my ass and levered me up while Bougie pulled me from above. I barely had my mask off before I began gushing.

"We saw triggerfish, parrotfish, rays, and a hawksbill sea turtle. Two of them." I struggled to unhook my BCD. "And a monster that tried to eat me."

"She ran into a giant grouper." Anton laughed and lifted the vest and my near-empty tank like they weighed nothing. "It was curious, nothing more."

"It scared the crap out of me."

"That ray was something, wasn't it?" Anton steadied me as I peeled off my flippers. "And those turtles. I've never been that close to them."

I beamed at him. "And there are approximately eight billion kinds of coral. I counted."

"I saw a humphead wrasse," Anton said to Bougie. "Untagged. We'll have to report to the marine ranger on D'Arros."

"That's one of the Outer Islands," I said. "Over a hundred miles away." Was he leaving already? My chest hollowed.

Anton helped tug my suit off my shoulders. "The humpheads are endangered, and they're monitoring the population around D'Arros. It would be a huge win to establish a population at Port Launay. He was a biggie too, about one and a half meters. I was following him, that's why I wandered off."

He brushed my skin, his hands cool and slick from hours in the water, yet heat bloomed at the contact.

"Nothing about the rest of my day is going to top this," I said. "We're having a staff meeting later at the spa to set up a date for the relaunch." I'd planned a small surprise Christmas party before the staff took a couple of well-deserved days off. "I'm really glad Bernard made me come."

Bougie cut his gaze to Anton, who laid our gear along the side of the boat to dry. "Bernard, huh?" Bougie said, putting the engine in gear. "Ready to head in, boss?"

Anton straightened and looked my way, blue sky bouncing off his reflective shades. "Have you been to Ros Lepa?"

"Yeah, a dozen times. The scenery is gorgeous, the trail is easy, and it ends right behind the hillside villa where I'm staying." It felt like an invitation telling him that, though I knew he wasn't looking for one.

"Why don't you drop Saba and me off at Ros Lepa," Anton said to Bougie, "and you bring our gear back to the Royale."

Bougie pushed up his sunglasses, blinking in disbelief. "You took a woman diving, and now you're giving me your dive bag?"

Anton's shoulders tensed. "I'll pack it. All you have to do is carry it. And if you don't want to touch it, ask Ferhad."

I scrubbed my hair into a messy twist, trying to parse out this exchange.

Anton wasn't a chauvinist, so why didn't he take women diving?

And when I'd openly, blatantly, drunkenly invited him into my bed in France, to my great humiliation, he'd looked as if he'd rather be anywhere else. So why the effort now to spend time with me?

Because I knew the island and he wanted to explore. Or pity. It could be pity. After I'd been cast as such a sad sack at dinner last night, poor, lonely Saba, on her own in the world.

"You can drop me at Ros Lepa." I turned my face into the wind, letting it soothe my overheated cheeks. "I don't need an escort. Then you guys can go on to the rest of your day."

"A survey dive to get some baseline info," Bougie said, "if that storm they're predicting for later rolls in."

"It'll go north of us," Anton said, checking and stowing the gear I'd used. "I want to see a pitcher plant." The wind riffled his dark hair, and sun gilded his chest and shoulders. All that warm, smooth muscle.

I looked away to strap on my sandals.

"They're farther up the mountain, along with the jellyfish trees," I snapped.

"Then I'll bet there's something else you can show me," he said.

He hadn't meant the innuendo, I was sure. Bougie would be falling over laughing if he did.

Anton was curious about the world. He wanted to explore a new place. I knew this place. That was all this was.

"You've been around the world," I said, facing landward as Bougie swung the boat wide.

"Haven't you seen everything?"

As always, the island sucker punched me with its beauty. The peninsula where Makarios sat didn't have the pearled sand beaches of other inlets, but a rocky shore, starkly gorgeous in its own way, baring the granitic bones of the islands, the only ones like it in the world.

"I haven't seen everything I want yet." Anton's voice whispered past my ear, his breath brushing the side of my neck. He was too close. "Not near enough."

I couldn't stop my shiver, but I could pretend I didn't know what he was talking about.

He pulled on a T-shirt advertising a dive shop in the Cayman Islands and strapped on his hiking sandals. He packed his dive bag with the laser focus I'd seen from him in France, an activity he'd performed a thousand times, and yet with precision and care every time.

I imagined him that intent, that careful with a lover. I couldn't believe he ever thought he would disappoint a woman.

Our time under the waves had been magical. I knew it was a bad idea—a terrible idea—spending more time with him above ground, especially in this paradise that seduced the senses everywhere I turned.

I wanted more time with Anton Olivier, yet I knew as much as I had, an hour, an afternoon, a night, it wouldn't be enough. I'd want more still.

Some called Ros Lepa the devil's staircase for the shape of the huge granite blocks descending into the sea, stepping stones for a creature of gigantic size. Local legends said ancient sailors had carved the staircase as a way of coming ashore, but they fought over who: the Phoenicians, the Polynesians, or some now-lost tribe.

Bougie drifted the boat expertly alongside the shore and Anton leaned over, staring into the water, then loosed a whoop.

"Get the net," he shouted.

Bougie scrambled to hold the boat in the rocking waves, while I grabbed the fishing net. Anton scooped a dark gray, rounded shape out of the froth of water pounding a low rock, then held up his prize.

"No way," Bougie cried. "You found a love nut. Your luck is the shit, boss."

"It's only the shell," Anton said. "The seed is germinating somewhere, let's hope. I always wanted a *coco de mer* shell. I thought I was going to have to buy one."

His face held that look of wonder again, the one the camera caught, the one that sold his show to a million viewers a week, many of them female.

"You have to have a license to sell them," I said without thinking. "I don't get why it's called the love nut, though."

Bougie raised his eyebrows, his hands shaping the distinct twin mounds of the double shell. Some said the *coco de mer* looked like buttocks. To me, it was unmistakably a woman's groin area, sometimes with a light dusting of hair tucked into the crevice to complete the resemblance.

"Why not call it the sex nut?" I argued. "If that's what everyone thinks when they look at it."

"Because the best sex is love, Saba," Bougie said. "Jeez, what kind of guys have you been with?"

I couldn't look at Anton. Not with my face blazing with embarrassment.

I swung my legs over the side of the boat and jumped onto one of the low, flat stones before anyone could stop me.

I'd already shimmied into my swim cover, a light cotton dress, and had my water and sunscreen in my palm fiber backpack, another find from a vendor in Victoria.

I could barrel back to my villa and hide my scorching face and be safely far, far away from Anton Olivier in a matter of minutes.

I landed wrong and my ankle turned beneath me. I caught myself and straightened, pretending to adjust my bag on my back. I refused to humiliate myself any further and let Anton see what I'd done.

"Turn around," Anton called as I sat on a rocky shelf, hammered smooth by water and wind. He aimed a small waterproof camera at me. I tucked my hands beneath my knees to anchor my whipping skirt.

"Don't I have to sign a release to be on your show?"

"This is for me." He stowed the camera into a pocket of his shorts, then hauled himself up with muscular ease to sit beside me.

"You were trying to see up my skirt," I said.

"I should be so lucky."

He stared out at the water. From here we would see the islands of Conception and Therese, spindled clumps of green rising from turquoise water, fringed with white sand. Clouds massed to the west, piling atop the horizon like more mountains.

"That's my dream," Anton said, pointing to a distant beach. "Live on an island of my own. Dive in the morning, swim all afternoon. Eat what I catch or pick from a tree. Sleep in a hammock whenever it's not raining."

"Alone?" I couldn't stop myself from asking.

"I'd rather not, but what woman would want such a simple life? They all want glamour and luxury."

Not me, I wanted to say, but it would sound like a lie.

I lived and worked at the classiest resorts. I'd made it a career. He'd never believe what he'd described was a fantasy of mine, to lead a simple, self-sufficient life.

I didn't want to be alone either.

"I'd make my living leading dive trips," he went on. "I like people. I like teaching them about the beauty down here, and to stop using the ocean like a drain for their garbage."

I scrambled to my feet, ankle twinging. "Would you take your wife diving? Bougie said you don't dive with women."

Probably because amateurs slowed him down or freaked out around big fish, like I'd done.

Anton's eyes crinkled as he helped me rise. His touch scorched me, again. It seemed this was going to happen every time.

"I don't dive with women who want it to be foreplay and try to flirt and get my attention when there's so much else to see."

"How annoying," I said, my voice dry as dust. "And if they're going to sleep with you anyway, why waste the air?"

I turned and started up the next step without looking, and my foot slid on a stone. I rocked, and Anton grabbed my waist and steadied me.

"Because diving is my favorite thing," he said, "and I want to share it with someone who enjoys it as much as I do."

I drew a deep breath. *Steady, Saba.* "Sorry Bernard saddled you with me."

"It wasn't Bernard's idea."

I swung to face him. "Do you mean…?"

He wasn't looking at me, but at the sky. He hitched his pack over his shoulder.

"I lied. That storm's not going north of us. We better hoof it, Saba."

I hadn't hobbled far down the sandy trail cutting across the top of the rocks before Anton noticed. "When did you hurt your ankle?"

"It's not bad," I said through my teeth. "I'll make it."

He swung his pack to his front, arms flexing. "I'll carry you."

"It's a mile," I protested.

"And you're going to limp all that way?" He turned his back. "Hop aboard."

"I'll make a crutch and—"

"Wrap your arms around me, Saba." He reached back for me. "And your legs. Nice and tight."

"I'm too heavy." My voice was muffled against his shoulder.

He was so warm, so firm. So strong.

He looped his elbows beneath my knees and hoisted me against him, my legs spread wide.

"You weigh about as much as a full scuba tank," Anton said. "Now, put your hands wherever you like, but don't mess with my nut."

I quickly gave up on the mortification and surrendered to the joy of riding on Anton's back, breasts pressed against his muscles, his beautiful lean body between my legs.

He didn't even seem winded when, halfway there, I said, "Stop a second."

"Need to pee?" He lowered me, and I immediately missed his heat.

I found my balance and stepped off the trail. "Come here."

His eyes lit with interest, then widened as I squatted and pointed. "Pitcher plant."

"No way." He grabbed his camera and snapped, grinning with glee. "It looks like a used condom, doesn't it?" he asked, admiring the green tube on its long stem.

I snorted. "Maybe to you." I was already ridiculously hot and turned on from having my lady parts pressed against his body with only the thin barrier of my swimsuit and his shirt between us. I didn't need the mental image of Anton Olivier, condom-clad.

I stood and looked at the sky. "We're not going to beat the storm."

"One more thing I want to do in the Seychelles." Anton beckoned me onto his back. "Get caught in the rain."

"What else do you want to do in the Seychelles?" I asked as I clasped my hands across his chest.

He squeezed my ass, and I yelped. "I'll tell you when we get to your place," he said.

The clouds chased us, low and near, and opened their torrents moments before we cleared the forest and reached the lane linking the hillside villas. Each sat tucked in a craggy swath of green overlooking the rocky private beach below.

Bernard had given me one of the newer suites, instructing me to try out all the new eco-friendly features and to make suggestions.

I pointed to my place, and Anton charged across the yard, turning to let me punch in the security code to the private gate.

Raindrops bounced off the patio, drilling the private pool as he sprinted inside.

We were both drenched and laughing when he stepped into the master suite where I'd left the curtain wide open to catch the tropical air, and now the scent of tropical rain.

He slid me down his body, slow and deliberate, then turned to face me. I stood within his arms, and he in mine.

I felt his arousal, thick against my belly, blotting out caution and sense. His skin was slick and cool and his eyes burned bright blue.

He dragged his hands from my hips up my sides, skimming my ribs, and leaned down to whisper against my lips.

"Say no if it's no." His voice was ragged and tight. "Just kill me now."

I'd stepped into a dream. A fantasy where Anton Olivier wanted *me*.

"It's yes." I anchored my hands on either side of his head and dragged his face to meet mine.

Finally, I was going to kiss Anton Olivier.

His mouth was lightning striking mine, a jolt that rattled me to my fingertips.

My heart slammed in my chest as I devoured him, and he me, the kiss urgent, searing, explosive.

I melted against him with a whimper, and then, in the next moment, yanked away as memory hit.

"You turned me down. On the beach in France. The night we went dancing."

"I never said no." The sky was dark with clouds, the room a quiet shadow. He swept his thumbs under my breasts, then moved his hands up. "You didn't give me a chance."

"I asked you—invited you back to my room—and you looked at me like…"

"Like I couldn't believe the incredible gift I'd been handed? I was sure you were teasing. You were the ice queen. All the guys joked about how they'd made a pass and you shut them down.

"Then you snuggled this incredibly sexy body up to *me*." He flicked his thumbs over my nipples, which hardened instantly.

Sparks flew to my belly, then dropped between my legs into a pool of fire.

"Trust me, in all the thousand million times I've reimagined that moment, I didn't stand there like an idiot. But I was stunned. I was afraid you were messing with me."

I pressed myself against him, dragging my mouth across the line of his jaw. "You *are* an idiot. Of course I wanted you. But I had to stand in such a long line."

"Then when it was finally my turn, when I snapped for the bait, you said no."

He crowded me toward the king-size bed, neatly made, crisp pillows plumped against the headboard.

"Out of the blue, you sucker punched me with your invitation, and then before I could say a word, you turned and ran off.

"No one knew where you went. And the next day, you were gone." He slid his hands beneath my swim cover and pushed it over my arms. He kissed me again, roaming his hands over all the new places bared to his touch.

I gasped and pressed into his touch.

I couldn't kiss him enough.

"Your face," I said, not sure why I couldn't accept my luck. Because the humiliation had cut so deep? "Your face said, 'Help, this weirdo. How do I tell her to go away?'"

He unhooked the catch of my suit and peeled it off me like he was unwrapping a present. "You didn't let me answer."

He laid me on the soft coverlet, then swiftly stripped off his shorts and shirts and lowered his body over mine.

That lean, bronzed body, all silken muscle and smooth skin. I floated my hands over every inch I could reach.

"I had to follow you all the way here," he said, "to tell you my answer is *hell yes*."

I stopped my hands in their long glide up his back. "I don't have condoms."

He sat back on his heels. Anton Olivier, naked and aroused, in my bed. He ran a hand along my calf. "We can find other ways to have fun."

I certainly didn't want to stop him. "I, um, have an IUD."

Oh, so sexy, but we were adults, and I was not drunk this time. We had to have the talk first.

He traced the crease of my knee. The light was dim from the clouds outside, veiling us from the rest of the world. "I had a physical before I came here. One of the government stipulations. Clean bill of health, if you're asking."

I let my knee fall to the side. "Then we're good."

He groaned and cupped my face to kiss me. "Oh, yes, please."

Anton Olivier, kissing my face, my neck. My breasts—he spent a lot of time there—then my belly, moving lower.

The storm hit in full force, the tops of the palm trees thrashing in the wind, almost as much as I thrashed in the bed as Anton brought me to pleasure again and again.

I thought nothing could surpass the sweet ecstasy of his mouth on me, but when he was finally done playing and slid inside, when our bodies joined, we came together like the rhythm of the pounding waves. Our storm crested and broke with the one outside, and I might have screamed his name.

We floated together as if underwater again, weightless, suspended, connected, breathing each other's air.

Eventually, when we calmed, I rolled to my side and he tucked himself along my back, resting one warm hand on my hip.

We watched the trees around the pool bend and dance, the water swish back and forth with the wind.

"What are we doing for dinner?" Anton murmured into my hair.

My heart jumped. He wasn't putting on shorts and leaving. I thought that was his signature move.

I tugged my bag from the floor and fished out my phone.

"I'm supposed to meet Bernard and the staff at the spa for—nope, meeting canceled."

I scanned the hurried set of messages with their several typos, sitting up in alarm.

"Bernard says the rest of them are trapped in the spa. The power went out, but they turned on the generator. He wants everyone to shelter in place." I scrolled down. "He texted the Royale. Ferhad said they didn't know where you were."

Anton laughed and took my phone away, tossing it on the nightstand. "Bougie knows where I am. I'm glad the others are safe, and I'm more than glad we're stranded here, all alone."

I leaned over him. "You planned this with Bougie."

His eyes lit as I straddled him, and he slid his hands to my hips. "Hoped. He probably thought my soggy ass would show up a long time ago, your handprint on my face."

I tried to roll away. "Anton Olivier scores again. To no one's surprise."

He brought me back, anchored my bottom over his groin. He was already swelling again. For me.

"To my great surprise, and delight. Saba Sweet," he whispered, nudging me. "Can our team score again?"

I laughed and surrendered. There was no doubt I wanted him. Our one night would be over soon enough, and I wanted to draw out every moment as long as I could.

What a night, though. The man was indefatigable.

Silently, I blessed the storm that made it impossible for us to leave, to do anything but be together.

Well past dinner time we rifled through my pantry and found crackers, cheese, a handful of nuts, and two bottles of wine in the tiny wine cooler in the kitchenette. I set our cheese plate in the alcove overlooking the pool, the hillside, and the beach below. Anton ventured to my patio and harvested the trees there, filling my arms with passion fruit, papaya, and an overripe breadfruit, black specks dotting the yellow diamonds of its skin, sweet enough to eat raw.

"You know what they say about breadfruit in the Seychelles," he said, spearing a chunk of the fruit. He nestled beside me on the couch, his shoulder warm and sturdy, as we watched the storm blow itself out. "Eat one here, and you will return to the islands."

"I'd return," I said, closing my lips around the fruit as he offered the fork to me.

"Or stay?" His eyes studied my face.

I shrugged. "That really isn't what my job is. I come for the short term, fix something, then I move on." If I'd ever worked in a place I wanted to stay, it would be Makarios. But somehow, I'd created a career that depended on my leaving, just when I got comfortable.

"You know what that's like, though," I said. "The short term."

He expertly cut and then pulled apart a mangosteen, exposing the segmented white fruit inside the brilliant purple shell. A surprise hidden within, like him.

I'd suspected there was another Anton behind the careless playboy façade. He was passionate about his diving and the ocean, and intensely committed to preserving the natural world and its wonders. He had a serious side that ran deep.

"I'm starting to think I want a home base," Anton said, handing me slices of fruit. "Or a home person."

He stared out the open wall, down the green-woven hill to the bay, where wind churned the water into wild spray. His face in profile was so sternly beautiful it hurt me to look at him.

Whoever Anton Olivier chose would be the luckiest woman on the planet.

"Don't you?" He turned those steel-blue eyes to me, and I caught my breath. Those eyes cut through my haze of fantasy. He was too perfect to be real.

"Nah." I occupied myself with arranging cheese slices on crackers. Nic had already pointed out my relationships were as short as my contracts. I wasn't ready to analyze why that was, especially with him.

"I tend to only look ahead to the next project." The confession felt hollow and small. I popped a cracker in my mouth to cover my unease.

Some people had what it took to settle down, but I didn't think that was in my genes. My dad had crossed the world for a job and found a wife, then spent his life pulled between two places. My mom had cut herself loose after Dad died and traveled wherever her whims took her. Moving around was in my blood.

Anton would move on from this night, and so would I.

"Plans for Christmas?" he asked me. "It's, what, two days away?"

"That reminds me." Some inner restlessness warned me to pull away, play it cool. "I need to light my Advent candle."

I'd found it at a market, a blue pillar marked with gold lines for each day counting down until Christmas. Once it caught, the small flame held steady. Looking at it made me happy. No matter what else was coming—and how much it was going to hurt to say good-bye to Anton—there was still Christmas.

"That's a neat tradition. We never had anything like that."

"How did you celebrate?"

He shrugged and poured us both more wine. "Dad was Catholic, Mom was Muslim, so they tried to teach us to be tolerant of everything. We went to Christmas Mass and fasted for Ramadan and donated to charity on Eid."

I sat beside him. "We used to have big Christmases. The whole family at our house with games and gifts. Mr. Mitchell from next door would dress up as Santa. But since my dad died..." We'd already gone over this. "My mom decided to stay in her ashram. She didn't even send a card. Maybe she'll call."

I sensed his gaze on me, looking too closely, so I picked up my wine glass and forced a bright smile. "Your plans?"

His eyes flickered and he looked away. "I might go to Morocco."

I hid behind my glass. "We heard your call."

He glanced my way, put his hand on my knee. "Don't look like that. It's not a booty call."

"None of my business if it is."

He sat up. "Do you honestly think I would go from you to someone else, a day later—"

"If you want to, who's to stop you?"

"You are so infuriating." He set my glass aside, stood, and

scooped me from the couch.

"Where are you taking me?" I squirmed, but not enough to make him drop me. I *wanted* to be in Anton's arms.

"I'm mad. I need to cool down." He marched outside to the patio, to the long sliver of private pool, shimmering turquoise blue. He dropped me in.

I came up spluttering. "This is…not warm."

"Serves you right." He splashed in beside me and yanked me into his arms. I wrapped my body around his. I wore only my swim cover, he his shorts, and both came off easily.

"I'll show you," he muttered against my neck, kissing his way down to my collarbone, my breasts.

"What?" I panted, floating against him, loving the incredible feel of the silky water and Anton's rough-soft hands on my body.

With the cool water teasing between my legs, then his firm length sliding inside, it took only moments for me to shudder and dissolve in his arms, clinging to him with low cries.

"Saba," he gasped, reaching for his own summit. "You're so…so—"

"It's you." I curled my arm around his neck, sobbing with pleasure as the wave threw me against him. "It's just you." I couldn't believe how responsive my body was with him, how intense the pleasure built.

Because this was paradise.

Because this time was stolen.

And it wouldn't happen again.

He whispered something in French, fierce and low, the words stuttering against my skin as his climax gripped him and his body pulsed inside mine. I thought he'd said *Be like this always*, but the thought swirled away as I followed him over the edge, the waves rocking both of us out of reality into something beyond, a place magical and perfect and pure.

***

I woke with a sandy mouth and sticky eyes, sun pouring through the open wall. The rust-colored curtains whispered in a light breeze, and the sky shone a hallowed blue.

My night with Anton Olivier was over.

I smacked my lips and groped for my phone on the nightstand. Ah, an excuse. "I have to get going."

"It's the day before Christmas." Anton lay on his back, one hand over his eyes. He reached out the other and rested it on my hip.

"And I have to work. I have to see what was broken by the storm, and plan how we'll fix it when the staff comes back after the holiday. We might have to push back our launch. There's the marketing and the budget, and the PR people and the—"

He rolled to face me. "It kinda feels like you're trying to get away from me."

No. I didn't want to be away from him for a minute. The sight of him in my bed, all that gorgeous skin and firm muscle, those eyes that cut straight through me—I wanted to stay right here. I wanted all this to be mine, for now and for a long time.

But I'd known what I was signing on to when I said yes. There was a queue for Anton Olivier, and I had a day, two at most, before it was time to move along.

Best to yank myself free now, quick and sharp and clean.

I swung my feet to the floor, stepping into a patch of bright sun. "Well, we're done here, aren't we?"

I heard his intake of breath behind me. "You're done?"

"I mean, this is the schedule, right? One night, maybe two, and then you move on? That's the plan."

"You think…" He narrowed his eyes and sat up, the sheet falling from his legs. I looked away. No fair using his luscious body to blot out my common sense.

"That's why you waited until that last night in France, isn't it?"

"What?" I padded to my closet, sorting through my few clothes.

"To come on to me. You knew you were leaving the next day.

Whether I said yes or not."

"Well, yeah. I stayed for my training dive, but my contract was up. And Bernard had made an offer." I kept my voice light. *Don't cling. Don't beg. Don't make him hate you.*

He rolled to his side, pulled on his shorts over his lean hips. His chest looked bigger when he was half-dressed.

"So you were always planning to leave."

"That's the job," I said, frustrated. Why was he stating the obvious? We both knew how this ended. It already hurt, and he didn't have to make it more difficult. "You do one night. I figured maybe it would fit your schedule, and—"

"And then you were *done*." His jaw set like the granite boulders anchoring the beach.

I whirled to face him, hands on my hips, linen camisole clutched in my fist. "You don't do relationships. I know that. Everyone knows that."

"You don't know what I wanted from you. With you." He swiped up his shirt from the floor and pointed at the bed with it. "If I had my way, you'd be in that bed with me at least until New Year's."

Dumbfounded, I tried to suck in air. "And then what?"

"I don't know. You're here for a while, I'm here for a while. There are hammocks on the beach. We could sit in a hammock and figure it out."

He was talking about days together. Maybe weeks. Yet I'd seen the brief relationships he'd had in France. I knew his reputation. "You don't..." I said again, then stopped. I'd crushed the shirt I meant to wear. "Why would I be different?" I whispered.

He ran his hands through his hair. "I don't know why. Because everything about you is different."

I stood there, stunned.

He was right. I'd waited until the last night in France to come on to him because, regardless of his answer, he was leaving.

I'd let him in last night, sheltering together from the wild storm because he was the great Anton Olivier and he didn't do relationships. We'd have fun and be done.

The end was already in sight, the clear break coming.

No attachment to fear. No separation to dread. No feelings that would twist and sour in my gut for days and years if I loved him and he left.

I *wasn't* different. I wasn't like the girls he dated, and I wasn't the kind of girl a man hung on to. My long string of exes attested to that.

I couldn't be left if I pushed him away first. My hands shook as I wrestled with my shirt.

He was changing the rules. He'd upset the entire playing board in one sweep, and I was supposed to run with the ball? I didn't even know what the goal was.

"I have to go to work and see what Bernard needs. Maybe we can hang out later, talk this out."

"Yeah. Sure. We can hang out."

He stomped into the sitting room, past the wide low couch where we'd snuggled for hours. The glasses of wine sat empty, a blood-red gleam in the bowls.

He let himself out of the gate, which swung quietly, mechanically shut behind him.

He was gone.

I had my one brilliant night with Anton Olivier, and it ended with shouting and agony.

I sat on my bed and let the tears pour into my cupped hands, salty as the sea.

***

Nic cornered me behind the reception desk where I stared at the screen of my tablet, watching the repair reports come in from the various parts of the property. Trees down, furniture tipped, a solar pane splintered by a falling coconut, a leaky window in one of the spa rooms. Nothing we couldn't fix.

Unlike my heart.

"Everyone says Anton stayed with you last night." Nic slipped around me to try to see my face.

No use lying about it. Resorts were like boarding school. Everyone slept with everyone else, and everyone knew about it. "Yep."

"You don't look like it was great." Nic tapped a pen on the desk.

"It was great." I sighed. "Better than great. We talked for hours. He made me food. We went swimming in the rain."

He'd shared his dreams, his fears, his family stories, tales of school and favorite family vacations. I knew more about Anton in twenty-four hours than some people I'd known for years.

"And how was the sex?"

I shifted on my feet, pleasantly sore from using muscles that hadn't been exercised in a while. "He's a finely tuned machine. You know how with most guys you fake it and take care of yourself later?"

"Um, no." Nic screwed up her eyebrows. "I make the man do the work. Jeez, Saba, who are these guys you've been with?"

"Not Anton." I sighed and tapped off my screen. "Anton does the work." I grabbed Zippy's carrot and moved toward her enclosure.

Nic followed. "And?"

"That's it. I have a job to do, he has a job to do. I wish he hadn't gotten angry with me for stating the obvious."

Zippy rustled and hauled herself toward us, the tortoise version of a smile on her nubby face.

Nic wouldn't stop. "What's obvious?"

Zippy bolted her carrot, then budged her head against my hand, exactly like a cat. I scratched under her chin, her skin worn and leathery soft.

"That it's a holiday fling. I'm one in a long line. I knew that back in France. It's a hookup. Nothing more."

I knelt to brush Zippy's shell free of the leaves and dust, so Nic couldn't see my face. But I wasn't fooling her for a minute.

"Bullshit," she said. "The way that guy looked at you at dinner?

And he said it. Out loud. He practically wrote it on a banner. He didn't make a play for you in France because he was afraid he'd disappoint you. But after you opened the door, the man got here as fast as he could."

"Don't." I folded my arms across my knees and dropped my head to my forearm. Zippy chewed on one of my curls, tugging my scalp as if she too were trying to bring me to my senses.

"Now he finds you're the one who's offering tours for one night only. He's gotta feel bummed about that."

"I don't know how to do the long haul, Nic," I mumbled into my elbow. "I screw it up every time. There's so much hurt, and ick, and resentment, and...I don't want to deal with it again."

"Do you want *him*?"

"Of course I do." I shot to my feet. Zippy reared her head in surprise. "He's—he's the most amazing man I've ever met. The most amazing man ever, in all of history. He's gorgeous, and funny and smart and *so* sexy, and he loves the water, and he punched a giant fish in the face for me."

I rubbed a hand over my face, smearing my tears. "I want him, and when I lose him, I want the wound to have nice clean edges so it heals fast."

"Saba." Nic tugged on one of my curls, her voice gentle. "*Tifi*. If you want him, and he wants you, then maybe it doesn't have to hurt."

I blew air out of my cheeks and jabbed the screen of my tablet. "It always ends in hurt. It's called life. Now can we talk about the Christmas dinner tonight? I don't want all of you cheated of a holiday. Then there are repairs, and the press releases, and—"

"Incoming at the helipad!"

Bernard charged onto the lanai, bald head gleaming with sweat, gold-rimmed glasses askew. With his dark ebony skin, filled-out upper body, and skinny legs, the man reminded me of a grape popsicle. He blew by, gesturing for us to follow. "Come on, Saba. You want to see this."

A heavy whirring rose above the trees, the distinct chop of helicopter blades. I didn't know we were expecting anyone.

I shoved my tablet in my bag, threw Zippy her head of lettuce, and ran after Bernard, who moved really fast for a popsicle.

The chopper was from the charter service, not the guy who made deliveries. I held back my whipping curls and waited outside the white marker until the landing gear bit the grass and the engine cut.

A roll-on suitcase popped out of the open door of the craft, followed by a slim, henna-dyed redhead with fair, freckled skin.

I was running well before she straightened, looked around, and then threw out her arms.

"Mom."

***

I sat on her bed while Mom hung her clothes in the small closet of my guest room. The open windows let in a warm breeze that gusted the sheer curtains. I couldn't look away from the small, silk-lined box in my hands. The handmade paper crinkled softly as I stared at faces I'd never see again.

"Merry Christmas, honey." Mom dropped a kiss on my head, then sat beside me.

"I'm so glad you came." I grabbed her hand. "But I didn't expect—" I couldn't talk through my tears. "I thought I left this picture in Thailand."

"You left it in Mississippi the last time you came to visit. I borrowed it."

I stared at the photo of the three of us, Mom, Dad, and me, taken at Ylang Ylang Beach Resort in Costa Rica. They'd come to visit the summer I interned there, one of our last family vacations before Dad got sick. Our wide smiles as we took our selfie by the pool, the wild green jungle behind us, promised we felt nothing but joy.

The frame held a mosaic of tiny trinkets from our vacations, from beach pebbles and coins to stubs from museum tickets. In one corner was embedded Dad's bronze pin from the University of Buea in his home country of Cameroon, where he'd spent several semesters as a visiting professor, sometimes taking us with him.

Tears dripped onto my hand as I traced the nubbed surface holding so many memories, all our best times together.

"I miss him so much, Mom." My voice rasped with the howl I wanted to let out.

She wrapped her arm around my shoulder. "He hated leaving you most of all, Saba. He made peace with leaving me, he knew I'd survive. But he'd have given anything for more time with you."

"Same here."

What I'd give to be able to call him and tell him I went diving and saw coral up close, and that I was nearly swallowed by a giant grouper. To tell him I'd finally met a guy who had the same steady presence, the same deep calm I'd always admired in my dad.

The tears fell faster. Mom pulled me against her shoulder. "Saba, honey. You can't think all guys will leave you because your dad did. It wasn't his choice to get sick and die."

"I know that." I leaned into her warm shoulder, feeling five years old again. "But it hurts so much, Mom. And it doesn't stop."

"You can't run from love because it might hurt you, baby. I've seen you do it over and over. The guy in Austria, the guy in Rome, that Turkish cutie who worked with you at the Dragonara in Malta. And what was the name of that boy in Japan? The one you were engaged to for five minutes?"

"Taiga. But I got that offer at Tanah Gajah in Bali, and he wanted us to stay in Izu. The commute would have killed us."

"So you left him."

"I—"

"Left." Mom nodded.

"Because it wouldn't have worked," I said weakly.

"Do you know that about this one? Anton? I talked to your friend, Nic, and she told me everything. I like that girl. And you know what else I like?" Mom shook her head. "That Anton. I started watching his show when you met him in France, and *honey.*" She gave a low wolf whistle. "That man is the entire package. Top of the line, grade A, one hundred percent pure—"

"He's certifiable, I agree. But he's thrown everything sidewise. I thought he was going to be a fun, *really* fun, one-night stand, and then he hinted he wants more time together, and I panicked. It wasn't pretty."

"And now you want more great sex?"

I strangled back a laugh. I couldn't remember ever having this frank of a conversation with my mother, certainly not about my sex life.

"Yes," I said, wiping my eyes. "But also, I want more of the *more.* I think. When I'm around him I feel..." I searched for words I'd never used before. "Lit up from the inside. Like I'm plugged into some energy source. When I'm with Anton, I feel like every part of me is alive."

"Then maybe you should tell him that." She pressed a kiss into my hair.

I leaned my head on her shoulder. Mom seemed softer, looser than I'd ever seen her, like her time in the ashram had lessened the clouds of worry and grief she'd always carried, even before Dad died. She moved like her skin fit her, like she wasn't afraid of being hurt.

Anton had that same grace, that confidence, that sense of being anchored to the earth.

"And then he decides he wants something else and leaves me, and then what?" I asked.

"You hurt for a while. You mope and write bad poetry, like when you were fifteen." I laughed and lightly slapped her arm. She smiled, then sobered. "You hurt a lot. For a long time. I'm not going to lie."

I sniffled. "But you met Sanjay. I have to say, I'm a little hung up on the jealousy. You get to find a new boyfriend, but I'll never get a new dad."

She nodded and squeezed me. "I know, honey. No one will ever replace your dad for me, either. But there can be new love. And if Anton isn't the ever after, then you keep going, and you find something, or someone else that makes you come alive."

I wiped my eyes. "So to fix this, I tell him how I feel?"

"He started, didn't he? So now it's your turn."

She squeezed me once more, then stood and walked into the main room cleaned from the previous night.

Everything about the place screamed of Anton.

The pool where we'd made waves.

The pillows where we'd lain on the floor playing mancala, and he captured more of my stones because he kept distracting me with kisses.

The bowl on the table piled with passion fruit and papaya. His bag in the corner with—

His bag. With his *coco de mer* nut inside.

I opened the sack and showed Mom. "He left this. I'll return it to him and apologize—"

Her laughter stopped me. "Oh glory, that's obscene."

"It's the world's largest seed, Mom," I said with dignity. "These trees are native to only two islands in the Seychelles. It is special, and important, and…" Her laughter got to me. "Yeah, it looks exactly like girl parts. That's why they call it the love nut."

She patted me on the shoulder. "Then go tell this guy you love him, you nut."

***

Nic agreed with my mom. I couldn't simply hand Anton his *coco de mer* shell and tell him I liked him. I had to put myself out there and do something big.

Both of these things went against the grain. I liked to have strict, clear boundaries and stay within them. Throwing myself at Anton Olivier was my version of leaping off a cliff without a net.

Bernard motored us along the coast toward the northwestern

archipelago jutting into the ocean, creating the inlet of Port Launay. I curled my fingers into my palm, sand embedded under my nails, wondering if my grand gesture would work.

We spotted Bougie, floating Anton's boat near shore, and Bernard let me out beside a palisade of thin-boled mangroves, their looping roots twisted like hieroglyphics.

Anton, in bright Lycra, stood on the beach, fiddling with a camera. Red crabs scuttled over my feet as I neared. Sun lit the crayon-blue sky.

Do this, Saba. Put yourself out there.

He lifted his head, spotted me, and stilled. I kept walking.

"I came to invite you, and Bougie, and, um, the whole team to dinner at the restaurant tonight. At Helios. It's not far from your villa, and we rescheduled the Christmas party, and—you should come."

"That it?"

"No." I pulled breath into my lungs, groping for courage. "I, ah, wanted to talk to you."

His mouth twisted. "Talk?" He pointed at the harness on the beach at his feet. "Then strap in."

I finally recognized the brightly colored fabric spread about. A parasail. And the harness meant—

"Uh, no thanks. I'll watch."

"I thought you said you wanted to hang out sometime."

I swallowed past a dry throat. "Yes. I'd like that."

He pulled on his harness, tugging buckles, closing clasps. "Then come with me."

My stomach slithered like water around those mangrove roots. "I'm not... I've never been parasailing. Heights, high in the air, tiny rope...that's not my thing."

His face was close. All of him was very close. I leaned toward him despite myself. He smelled of salt, sunblock, and sea.

"You've come to tell me you changed your mind and want to spend time with me after all."

"Um. Yeah." I squeezed my fingers, surprised he read me so easily. Was I that obvious?

"But on your terms." He yanked the straps tight around his waist. "You'll tell me your expectations. And somehow, I'll disappoint you. I won't be what you want."

"*You* are what I want," I blurted. "Just you."

"Then come with me." He held out the second harness, a bright, hot challenge in his eyes.

I tugged at the hem of my tennis shorts, terrified. But if I stayed on solid ground, tried to negotiate a set of safe, clear terms, I'd lose my chance to be with Anton.

And I wanted to be with him.

I took a deep breath and stepped into the harness.

"If I have a heart attack and die up there, you have to explain it to my mother."

He brushed his hands over my body, much more than was necessary to make sure my harness was secure. By the time he was done, my whole body glowed.

"Do you trust me?" he asked, meeting my gaze.

"Yes."

"Then you know I'm not going to hurt you." He spoke softly, his head bent near my ear.

I gulped. "Those aren't mutually exclusive. I can trust you and you can still hurt me." This harness could be really tight, and I could still fall out of it.

He ran a finger beneath a shoulder strap, above my pounding heart. "Step into it," he said, "and let it catch you. It's like falling in love."

Bougie started the boat and winched up the sail. Anton took my hand and tugged me forward. The chute lifted, swallowed a billow of air, and the jolt brought me off my feet. I screamed, and Anton laughed.

"Incredible, isn't it?" he shouted.

I dug my fingertips into his hand. "Like I might die, at the same time I never want it to end."

"That's how I felt all last night."

The rope unfurled and we leveled out, soaring like birds.

The Seychelles spread beneath us, smaller islands curled like green hedgehogs in beds of turquoise, cyan, and deep blue. Green coral reefs shimmered beneath the surface.

Clouds stretched thin as smoke near the horizon. Morne Seychellois rose to our left, stubbled with green, and other boaters waved as we passed above them.

The whole world belonged to us.

"Why'd you spook?" Anton asked me.

He held the camera to his eye, panning the scenery below and around. The shape of his face, carved against a background of lapis lazuli, pained me with its beauty.

"Is that thing on?"

"Not audio. I'm recording footage for the report. Maybe for the show later, if the government lets us."

I gripped my hands around the straps holding me to the sail, these thin pieces of thread and cloth. "My mom will tell you I push people away so they can't hurt me. Your basic self-protection reflex. I'm not a fighter, so I flee."

"And what would you say?"

The sway of the harness dangled me over nothing but water. A long, hard fall.

"I'm used to the short-term projects. Not sure how I'd do on a longer assignment," I said.

"So why am I different?"

My question, turned back at me. I didn't know how to explain it. Because with him, *I* was different. I was willing to take the heartache I'd feel if I lost him for the joy of the time we'd have.

For him, I was willing to risk my heart.

Bougie headed toward the small cove that belonged to Makarios, the small private beach below my villa.

Anton started to laugh.

On the beach in letters as high as I could make them, not yet lapped by the tide, lay my declaration for all the world to see: SABA IS NUTS ABOUT ANTON. For punctuation, I'd used his *coco de mer* nut.

"For real?" he shouted.

I gulped. "If I survive this, yes."

Bougie swung the boat around the cove and winched us down, fast but easy. Following Anton's example, I bent my knees and we stepped onto land.

Anton caught the chute and swiftly bundled it while I grappled with my straps. He scooped me out of the harness into his arms and gave me a kiss that stole my breath.

"How long do I have?" he murmured, kissing my jaw.

I gripped his arms. "I don't know. As long as it's good, I guess?"

His eyes burned as he looked at me, knowing, passionate, triumphant.

"We'll work on that answer," he said, and then his tongue was in my mouth, his body wrapped around mine, and my head spun as my knees dissolved and I was weightless again, floating, surrendered, in the only place I wanted to be.

***

My Christmas Eve party was a smashing success. I wore the dress I'd ordered from Míe, an atelier I'd found based in Lagos, Nigeria, that was my new go-to for ethically and sustainably made resort wear. The blocky indigo print looked great with my tan, the linen maxi-length skirt swirled seductively around my legs, and the bikini-cut bodice, held in place by a few straps, bared a whole lot of skin.

The dress was worth every penny when I saw Anton's expression.

We feasted on barracuda grilled with garlic and ginger, coconut curry, a satini made of shaved golden apple, and breadfruit baked in coconut milk and sugar for dessert. The palm wine flowed, and I passed out bonuses to the staff.

Bernard gave a toast that made me struggle not to cry.

Anton walked Mom and me back to my villa, his hand tangled in mine as we strolled through the verdant, velvet dark, and my heart tumbled around in my chest.

What if the reality didn't live up to the fantasy of the first night?

What would my mom think of us sharing a room?

When we got inside, she winked, firmly slid shut the door to the guest bedroom, and turned on her white noise maker.

The second night was even better than the first, because we knew each other better, and we could take our time. We didn't have to hurry to fit everything in, and I didn't have to worry how to end things in the morning.

There would be another night. And another. And another.

Christmas morning, Anton came with us to mass at Saints Peter and Paul in Port Glaud, a snug little church of gray brick trimmed with white, the interior draped with festive bunting against the bright yellow walls.

Mom and I lit candles for our loved ones, another of our Christmas traditions.

Anton seemed to know all my favorite songs, and his voice, strong and steady, sent vibrations deep inside my chest.

After church, Mom went home, and Anton and I traded our church clothes for swimsuits. We hiked to Sauzier waterfall where we paid our rupees, climbed the rocks, and splashed in the pool, the water thick and soft as a Berber rug.

Anton picked starfruit from a tree and we lounged next to a small pool, enjoying our picnic. Light filtered through the palms, otherworldly and magical, and I blinked back sudden, surprising tears.

This couldn't be real. Me here in this magazine-shoot paradise with this camera-ready man. It didn't look like anything that could fit in the real life of Saba Sweet. It had to be holiday madness, a fantasy bubble that would burst and leave nothing behind.

Yet it didn't feel fragile. It felt easy. *Right.*

Anton was surprising and funny and exciting, yet as he held out a hand to help me up and we walked the trail back to my villa, our steps fell into rhythm as natural as the tide, as sure as the circling sun.

Did I dare step off the boat into unknown waters, or was I going to cling to dry land?

Nic's family knew how to throw a Christmas party, and they'd been going at it all day by the time we arrived. Music swam through the air, drinks spilled from cases and coolers, barbecued meat and fish smoked on the grill, festive dishes and every kind of fruit tumbled like jewels across decked-out tables.

When it grew dark, I withdrew to a quiet spot on the Grand Anse beach, stepping around the lit tents and small fires. It was too much, all the joy and laughter. Nic's big family teasing and wrestling and eating and looking out for one another. I needed to catch my breath.

Behind me, under a canopy fringed with red and green lights, Mom danced with Bernard. She laughed in a way she hadn't laughed since my dad died. She'd told me more about Sanjay, her new boyfriend. I told her I'd like to meet him.

Mom seemed sure of herself, grounded, at ease. Maybe that was Sanjay, or the ashram, or both.

I studied the constellations, a whole new sky. One star shone brighter than the others.

"Everything's so different, Dad," I whispered, my chest aching.

The star winked, and I could feel him beside me. This man who had traveled the world and braved an entirely foreign culture to be with the woman he loved.

That doesn't mean you can't be happy, the star said.

My dad would tell me to be brave. To take a risk. To enjoy the good times while they were here.

Anton walked toward me, loose-gaited and relaxed, and that achy, anxious feeling in my chest turned and settled like a small animal settling into its burrow.

Here was a man at home in his body, whatever the surroundings.

And what a body. His T-shirt boasted a huge print of Bob Marley's face, silk-screened in red and green, and his cargo shorts and sandals showed off his lean, strong legs.

I wanted to put my mouth on every inch of his body I hadn't yet tasted, and revisit the places I had.

He dropped down beside me on the sand and held out a beer. "Not signature cocktails at a five-star restaurant."

I took the bottle, hard and smooth, sweating from the cooler. "I don't need five stars all the time. I like a beer and a hammock on the beach, same as anyone else."

He turned his face to me, firelight dancing in his eyes, and kissed my forehead. "Please don't be saying that so you can get close to me and then try to turn me into some playboy celebrity your model friends can be jealous of."

I trailed a finger, cool from the beer, across his collarbones. "I can and have eaten merguez every day, and I *love* truffle fries."

He pressed his face into my hair. "I can't believe you're so perfect."

"Same goes for you." I wanted this dream to never end.

Anton Olivier propped his arm behind me and I learned against his chest, putting a hand on his knee. He felt solid. Real. Like he wasn't going anywhere.

We stared at the immense, swooping stars, and that tiny, sabotaging voice whispered in my head, echoing his question from earlier. *How long?*

"Not to rush things." Anton took a swig from his beer. "But I want to get married on a beach, then have a big blowout barbecue, like this."

I choked on my drink. "You *are* rushing things."

"Two kids, boy and a girl. And we give them family names. Maybe name the girl somehow after my grandma and your mom, who, by the way, gave me her blessing."

"You won her over quickly."

He bobbed his head to the music. "And the family stays together.

None of this one of us leaving for long periods for a job. We get a tutor or whatever, but we go together."

He draped his forearm along my chest, and I snuggled closer. "Bernard asked me to run Marakios. He wants me to stay and be the real manager. I'm thinking I might take a couple more jobs, to get more experience with places like this, and then come back."

He drank his beer, nodded. "I could lead dives. And we'd never run out of ideas for shows. Hey, want to do New Year's in Morocco? My sister's flying in."

"Your sister?" My heart squeezed.

We were meeting family already. Big step.

"Yeah, she called that night at dinner. She told my parents to fly in too. Surprise for our grandparents."

I laughed. "We all thought that was a booty call."

He squeezed my shoulder. "All I want is right here."

"For Christmas?" I teased.

"For always."

My chest swelled, as if it could grow large enough to fit all this, the beach, the celebrating people, this beautiful and utterly unique island, the swaths of stars. I held out my beer bottle and he clinked it with his.

"Merry Christmas," I said, then remembered. "I didn't get you a gift."

"Yeah, you did," he said softly, and kissed me, and I was twirling inside those stars, caught in the heaven of Anton's arms.

Love is always worth it, Saba, Dad-star said to me.

I agreed.

ABOUT THE AUTHORS
Elle Wright

Elle Wright has been writing stories since she was a child, which led her to a career in journalism. She enjoys reporting life as much as making up a world she can control. She lives on the east coast of the United States where most of her large, noisy family resides. When she isn't in front of her computer, she loves to travel, garden, hang out with her dogs, and take in the brisk sea air that she's told is supposed to help calm her. She's been testing that theory for a while now.

CONNECT WITH ELLE:
IG: @Elle_Wright_Writes
FB: /elle.wright.1460

Misty Urban

Misty is a fiction writer and medieval scholar. While her academic and creative nonfiction deal with monstrous women and motherhood, in her historical fiction and contemporary romances she likes to reward her ambitious, rule-breaking heroines with handsome heroes and happy endings.

She lives in Iowa with a handsome park ranger, two other budding authors, and a heavy collection of books.

Connect with Misty:
website: mistyurban.com
fb : /authormistyurban
IG:@authormistyurban

TT: @misty.urban.writes

www.BOROUGHSPUBLISHINGGROUP.com

If you enjoyed this book, please write a review. Our authors appreciate the feedback, and it helps future readers find books they love. We welcome your comments and invite you to send them to info@boroughspublishinggroup.com.

Follow us on TicTok and Instagram, and be sure to sign up for our newsletter for surprises and new releases from your favorite authors.

Are you an aspiring writer? Check out www.boroughspublishinggroup.com/submit and see if we can help you make your dreams come true.

Love podcasts? Enjoy ours at:
www.boroughspublishinggroup.com/podcast.

www.ingramcontent.com/pod-product-compliance
Lightning Source LLC
Chambersburg PA
CBHW021113130626
46554CB00002B/671

Assemblage

Assemblage

by

J.M. Weeks

You wanted to know.

Table of Contents

If I Search For You

What are you?
Are you in the cool breeze
that moves through the hills
        in the morning?
In the intricate design of a leaf,
or a spiderweb in the sun?

I have eyes that see, and ears that hear.
I search for you in mountaintops,
and there you are resting
in views stretching forever.

I saw you in the eyes of my child;
        in innocence, love, and purity.
Are we closer to you by time,
or do we forget you the longer we're
        here?
Do we forget that you are with us?

I listen to you and I hear you;
when I try to, I can.
In every small world,
in every large world.
From minute to minute,
from hour to hour.
If I search for you,

I find you.

Hibiscus

I was thinking
for the sake of long ago.

Dim-light shadows,
curtains drawn;
fake wooden floors.

Intoxicated comfort;
wash away the days.

Midnight porch talk,
cobwebs on the
window panes.

Fractured sunlight,
little house out in the pines.

Cicada rhythms,
and the bright light
starry nights.

If I belong here,
some of this belongs to you.

All the ghosts we've known,
and the Hibiscus in bloom.

October 30th, 9:10 P.M.

We were ghosts in shadows
while we walked in beach sand.
I saw you lean over in new frames—
so many stars adorned your head.

You don't care much for the rules.
Your rhythm is the lapping of water,
a countdown as time will pass.
Your prayers still ascend to heaven.

While she played the strings and sang,
I lay curled close to her hourglass,
and hummed to the cleansing Gulf wind.
Her unbound heart was all around me.

Looking Out from Matanzas Beach

Today I said a prayer for peace.
I've been at the bottom of that ocean—
off the shelf, and into the trenches.

I'm leaving now—looking for
something rare and unknown;
something I couldn't find before.

On the Edge of a Thunderstorm

Raindrops patter—one, two, three;
begin to fall in the deep green wood.
Rumbling, roaring in the distant sky.
All else is silent—not a bird chirping,
as all creatures hold breath in pause.

Picture it—the distant gray,
moving slowly into the panorama.
Rain and flash! One, two, three.
Dark blue and grey—a violent sky.

Flash and bang! Heart pounds!
One-two-one-two-one-two-one-two...

Nothing can stop a thunderstorm.
Nothing can stop its creep and crawl;
its nightmare approach.
You thought you were safe...
Now your future held in hands
        unknown.

Dream #1

You are not my first,
though you may be my last.

Our final picture was
a kiss in the autumn rain.

Saw you last in darkness—
your porch in the winter night.

You waited until I was gone
and you slowly closed the door.

Autumn Flowers

Her hands clasped
the dried flowers
of fall's first wave.
The cosmic mixtures
of the equinox;
purple ∫ white ∖ yellow ∫ gold.

Just as the lines of her hands
held the very truths
that we must come to know.
We must walk in winter's shadow...
and find our weary way,
though winter's end is very far.

Dark December

I remember a dark December
withered leaf and smoking cinder
chilled me as the winter nearer

I remember a dark December.

set me free, avoid the triggers
lonely heart, the only danger
purple sky and full moon silver

I remember a dark December.

wishing well, the stars I wonder
wake the giant from his slumber
changing story by the numbers

six and seven not a dozen.

I remember a cold, cold winter
rumors like a spark to tinder
journey through a dark, dark desert

sparks are flying—cold, cold winter.

came to me a dream the other
night my hand upon your shoulder
felt just like I didn't know you

blessed are the broken hearted.

wishing well, the stars I wonder
wake the giant from his slumber
changing story by the numbers

say one thing and do another.

Sinking Stone

Tonic clonic, emotive—
can't— be— helped.
O— C— D.
Control what you can,
for all that you can't.
I'm fine...
Just finished—just fodder.

I'm like a sinking stone.

"You'll find a way!"
I still need you—
Electric!
You cracked my mind,
and I am changed—
Cold empty room...

Unchanging like a stone
Take it as a sign.
May God rest my bones.
Moving on—
Pick it up!

Gravity and time
have not tamed my mind
through the years.

The Fig Tree

The fig tree tells us what is to come.
It's the first to drop its leaves
when fall is still just a rumor.
It's the first to put them on
when spring is undecided.

The fig tree is at its best in summer,
giving shade from the hot sun.
In the cool where birds rest,
its sweet perfume hangs in the air;
just like honey and calm.

In late June our tree bears fruit.
We use hooks to pull branches close;
we pick figs and eat them until
        our stomachs hurt.
This for two weeks, as our daily event;
as the summer doldrums settle in.

I love to watch my children play
        under the fig tree.
They laugh, and jump, and plan in
        loud conversations.
Chasing chickens and climbing
        branches.
Large, velvety, fanned leaves in rich
        green—
roots and shoots, and new growth.

It's September now and I watch them
        fall; one, two, three—drop.
In a month a cool wind will blow
and the branches will be empty—bare,
        and jointed like skeletal bones.
All the while, dormant and waiting to
        wake again.

Assemblage

He faces as they walk away...
Is it wonder or something else?

The Atlantic won't give today.
Sloshing and wrecking
in black and white—
all the mist and foam.

My God! So cold!
How the tracks cross...
How tracks cross in distance,
as they walk away...

We, within the rush and roar
of wind and tide.
There is chaos out in
the whitewash waves.

Brutal Compass

It was in all the things we didn't know—
you held spring leaves and glanced;
your posture so telling in distant time,
yet I was too ignorant-young to really
      see.

We made quests and journeys inland;
into the hinterlands to map our lives.
"If you never bought it, why did you
      come?"
I worked for something better than that.

Sometimes work is not enough,
contrary to what I've been told.
Especially on the day when the truth
      comes forth.
Our hearts a brutal compass to lead
      the way.

Rare Moment

I saw you for the first time,
while you walked in winter grass.
We didn't go near the water,
and I think that it was best.

We couldn't be pushed in directions—
We couldn't be pulled by tides—
We were unto our own.
I broke the fear that I was holding to,
        and put the old order to rest.

All I knew were your eyes and the
        moon—
and the far reach of Live Oak branches
that rested high above your halo.
And the night was clear blue,
like your image—your lips like ruby.
And I loved your stillness;
your softness, and your warmth.

You saw me for the first time
as we stood in the kitchen
        in quiet breaths.
I could hold you now as something
        close.
And we prayed, and I wondered—
just as God's love is wonder,
        like a million stars,
and the touch of your hand.

While It Rained In Tampa

At the time I just couldn't take anymore.
Another afternoon of horrifics...

It was the darkness of my fear state,
through the unknown all around me.

It was in the hotel's neat, clean edges,
though it still smelled like piss and
       bleach,

and I felt fear—
I felt fear as a taste in my mouth...

I felt the sinking sickness
that no medicine would cure.

It was in the instructor's look...
that he thought I was a bastard

for leaving so often,
so I could go crumble to my fear,

as raindrops fell hard,
splashing and not cleansing,

because I felt nothing could cleanse me,
though I prayed that this storm would
        pass quickly.

Glory, Glory, Hallelujah!

Glory, glory, hallelujah!

Beware!
At last the November drum roll.
Hear the song and tribal march—
fly your flags and banners too!
Spectacular, tepid pantomime,
with writing on the walls;
loud and clear.
No one is reading the room.

How can tomorrow ever come?
You say it will be, but how?
I don't believe it...
Within a year, a slave to solace.
No voice to react and no dream to see.
DIVIDE!!
The motto and mantra.

Say peace and love, but you politic first,
for love and unity and money war?
With weaponized words—point of a
        gun.
Firing assumptions as we fall to
        confusion.
Minute by minute, we live lives in
        minutes.
We don't want the same?

Glory, glory, hallelujah, amen!

Mountain Song

Sun comes rising now
out my window.
Tree horizon
in morning shadows.

Think I'll walk down,
which way the trail goes.
Try to forget
the things I don't know.

Rhododendron
hangs above the trail.
Streams a'shimmer,
forest's veil.

Purple mountains,
blue and green.
Open mind
and set me free.

Walked so many
crooked miles.
See the clouds move
through the sky.

Of creation,
what lies ahead?
Spider web
so intricate.

Is it true

that we're alone?

One day the blackbirds

pick our bones.

Fighting Back

He decided to throw his skateboard
through your windshield.
He might not get it back,
but it's bound to prove a point.

Angels

Boiled and burned—
skin melted.
Red, raw, and oozing.

It smelled like dead skin
and body odor
as I sat in the shower—
everyone looking.

She smiled and said,
"It's surgery."—slam!!

The verdict.
          The sentence.
                    The fear—

And I felt so low to the bottom...
Then an angel held my hand—
So many—they had flames at their feet,
and showed me love and compassion,
like no one had shown in so long.

They brought me back to the surface.

7:00 in the Morning

These old bones are turning blue.
A month's remittance is all I have,
with scandals draped in flowers;
with dried and cracked hands—
Cover your lips against a kiss,
with sunken eyes that won't look on.

Only time will tell;
it's in all the simple notions.
Something we all go through.
If I only had a dollar...
If I only had decent looks...
But I only have this broken car,
and I am only what you see.
There's nothing more.

Chrysanthemums line the bed
where you lay in the winter.
Spring and fall don't know.
Summer is for lovers,
but now it's cold.
Most of my mornings are wasted
on sickness of the gut.

With no enthusiasm, I live on.
Sitting in the cold car,
waiting for something to happen.

Dream #2

I met you again at the after party.
They asked me to have a drink, and
laughed while you sat at the table.
You wore a black dress and crossed
          your legs.
There was no sense in keeping it a secret
          anymore,
so I leaned over to kiss you, as you
          would kiss me,
and your kiss turned into a meditation;
an opening of the spirit into cosmic
          expanse.

The Audience

I stand before the audience everyday—
before the eyes looking, seeking.
What is this, exactly?
The oceans, and forests, and deserts;
all wanting for order and direction,
for explanation in ages of question.

Yet I am only one...
and I realize the weight,
so I just put on my faces.

Positivity and integrity at forefront:
the expectation.
Though I want to be as they are.
I want to share with them as they do.
To step aside from the course, if not
       just for a moment.

When This Ends

When this ends
you don't
have to be alone.
You don't have
to go back
into the unknown.

I do suppose
I dread it...
Just please see
that I hope
you will rise
so high above.

Marrow Deep

My love for you runs marrow deep,

like the veins of quartz in the mountain
      rocks.

Like streams that disappear from
      sight in forest undergrowth,

though they meander forward and carry
      the whisper of your names.

Homesick

It was quiet at the pool house now;
Southern accents subdued and settled,
and the quiet breath of relief when any
      event is over.

The teenagers still played in the pool—
this was their world, so I wandered
      the yard of tall green grass,
and down to the mud-water pond.

Ducks and catfish, poison ivy, and clay,
with the stench of mud and the hug of
      Georgia heat.
I felt the lump of loneliness in my
      throat.

Back at the pool house, I was with a
      family of faces, but none a home.
And too sick to swim in the empty pool,
too sick to fish or enjoy—to make new
      friends.

This deep blue sadness for home, or for
        people that I missed;
something I've pondered for the
        duration of life,
made known to me when I was ten and
        far away.

Luckily, my happy uncles talked to me—
        projecting love and warmth.
So I came around and settled down,
but I still counted the days until I could
        go back.

The Conversation

Surprised by the call—
we talked of religion,
of Appalachia and Rumors.
So I realized then,
that I might get to know you.

I slow-paced the yard—
I felt like a fool...
I explained broken ideas...
but you listened.

The sun started to sink;
it was the last of summer,
and your eyes shined
through distance and airwaves.

Your warm voice
gave me a home,
though I had not
felt at home for so long...

Dream #3

Came to me in a dream,
left me in a tangle...
Your face against mine—
neck entwined - ALL HEART

I felt your love for once;
you have a tender soul.
I didn't want your pity.
I wanted you—

Why do you stay if you're unhappy?
I would be "for" you.
Your straight teeth and locked up mind.
Where's the missing key?

Why suffer all of this indirection?
Now you come at me from all four
          corners.

Psalm

The psalm on my refrigerator
sits pinned while no one reads it.
I could've been more faithful,
as I walk by everyday,

yet by open doors and alignment,
she found just what she needed.
Blessing the thought and presence;
she blesses the synchronicity,

and understands God in ways
that I do not claim to know.
"I should not want,
for I lie down in green pastures,
and she restoreth my soul".

The Bridge

It's a long bridge across the bay,
In the tepid fall twilight.
Pastel glow with sun sinking low;
The water's gray sparkle-shine,
Opening the door to a new world.

Because Our Love

I walked in distance from my son,
as I tried to tackle what I might face.
He's always been about twenty yards
       behind me,
for some reason that I could not know.
I wish he could understand what eats
       at me...

I saw Mr. Smitt sitting in his truck;
all the age, and the rust, and the dust,
while he sat listening to old music—
it gave me some sort of peace.
A soundtrack—my prayer and a last rite,
before time propels you to whatever it
       holds.

I imagined he must've heard this song
with his father—whether it be true or
       not...
that maybe it connected the distance
       between them.
A message through the music...

to face the haze and dirt—
the reality of the beginning of a day.

I just hope they will know me,
for what I am and not what is said.
I hope they will know me for what is
       good,
and forgive me for my weaknesses.
I hope that they love me as I love them,
because our love, we cannot forget.

She Was Gone

We played drums and drank spirits,
smoking on humid summer nights;
uncontrolled and hedonistic—chaotic.
She could no longer hold her pain.
They lay like ghosts in back rooms.

The disease slowly took her life away.
We saw her fade and disappear to dust.
You said they opened the windows
        to let her spirit float away.
Curtains flowed in spiritual breaths,
        and she was gone.

————————————————————>

Elizabeth

Elizabeth slept curled on the seat,
as we drove home on Interstate 10.
They just buried his poor mother
in the Tallahassee clay.

She was precious and whole;
the world had not taken her yet.
She was at peace and dreaming,
just as I'd seen her asleep in the grass.

Until It Has All Played Out

Do you know where your white crosses
      are?

Prayers that seem to go into an abyss of
      infinite expanse?

I will just meditate on the silence
      instead.

I woke up writing, listening to the
      fringes;

listening to someone talk about a
      Confederate Jesus.

I have no qualms about the pure
      insanity of this world.

In the morning, I see the wear in my
      face.

The feel the wear in my heart nerves, yet
exist in perfect clarity.

I feel the alt-reality that plays out on
the screen in front of me.

Or like I'm in a tunnel with no light at
the end.

I stomp and stumble in the dark, feeling
my way in some direction.

Where it goes, I may never really know,
until it has all played out.

Embers in the Roots

Rain may kill a flame,
but it won't put out
the embers that are
deep within the roots.

The Clouds Began to Part

Steam rose off the water,
while raindrops splash.

The clouds began to part
in the day's last light,

while aqua-blue strands
reached out into tree lines.

The sun and palm
glowing in perfection.

Anarchy Love

I'm ready to write now—

You left your Bible.

You hide what you think.

I've hidden myself.

Do you see the deep cut
      lines of my hand?

You can't know the silence
      of this house...

Options that are impossible;

Tongue cut off for speaking.

Where do you go?

Your chaos and anarchy—

Your dying love.

I feel sorry as your mistake.

So much rhetoric.

About that?

I will give you nothing.

Spirit quest and gone—

Shattered mirror

In fragments,

A crash to the floor—

Your anarchy love.

For the Light of You

It's for the light of you
that I must remain,
and I remember this
in the quiet of night,
in the low light shadow-glow.

In feelings that run deep;
deep and dark blue.
In silent stillness,
after everyone has gone—
your memory as a light
        I still can't believe.

Untitled

I saw a bear in the road
as I talked to my father,
and the road looked different—
while the full moon set,
and a comet fell home.

I thought it humorously prophetic,
so the next day I cut my hair.
I painted my face in shadows.

———————————————

You are the slate-grey eyes
of early winter morning.
You are black rivers branching;
the steam off the water
in half moon darkness,
and December's freeze.

How many years?
How many years have past?
Yet you come to me as a ghost—
an energy that never sleeps.

White-Hot Heat (Hampton Blues)

Summer so hot to see wavy lines—
they call it refraction.
Like white-hot heat,
it pulls from the asphalt,
cracked and worn by the ages.

Afternoon to evening;
the black serpent makes his way
through tall green grass from wood line.
The many trees, gray with painted faces;
old and gnarled—rough with wisdom.

Weeds grow high against yard junk:
broken cars, lawnmowers, and twisted
        metal.
To stop the rot, and all of its madness...
While mud and sand splattered on the
        sides of houses,
the windows and screen doors shut,
while rain storms move away—
steamy, hot, humid night.

Street lights flicker and glow in
       yellow-orange.
Resonance of creaking screen doors,
and humming air conditioners
against the high pitched sounds of
       crickets and frogs—
the summer night's song.

Stop motion gas stations come alive—
they smoke and cough with leather
       faces.
Conjectures and steady boredom—
Save us from the ghosts of this town,
from the ghosts of this town and all that
       went wrong.
While up in the heavens, heavy with
       haze,
heat lightning flashes and flickers.
A train makes a solemn call—
static, sweltering summer night.

An Old Friend

You are gone and now you can't see...
How do you feel about that?
You can't see our age, or bring the room
        to life with laughter anymore.
You were bright and young and eager to
        prove,
and I remember you so—it wasn't long
        ago.
"You should've never done that."
What will your father say?
Don't you remember all of the adventure
        of life,
when we camped among the pines and
        palmettos,
in the deep, dark woods watching for
        headlights?
I don't know about you—why?
I always thought you out to impress,
but now I know that you would pull the
        trigger.

Lotus Flower

She's a Lotus flower
and I lost my mind.

I can't remember my way
back home anymore—
nor do I care...

You're Not So Innocent Anymore

The problem of it all is...
she worries that the world is falling
       down.
She says, "First they'll track you and
       then they'll bring you in."
Because the system breaks and fails to
       protect.
Never getting closer to the truth—
living in the midst of a putsch.
I'm not wary wise—just shy of paranoid,
and I know how it is—they watch us all.
I'm told to watch what I teach my
       children,
yet, they will see it all.
Compiled, and profiled, and filed—filed
       away,
and now you're not so innocent
       anymore...

Why should I pledge myself when the
        kids don't even believe it.
I only remember the words when I'm
        with the group—robotic.
And how many have died for the words I
        can't remember?
But I was able to buy a house, and a
        brand new car
on the might of an empire in a different
        name;
in the glaze that we cover all that is
        dark.

At what point do light and dark emerge
        as light?
At what point do light and dark emerge
        as dark?
At what point is opportunity an
        expense?
At what expense is my soul?

Weedon Island

There are remnant foundation stones
left in the sand dunes at Weedon Island.
And piles of oyster shells from an
          ancient people,
where the sun can reflect golden off the
          palm.
All the while, she makes shapes with her
          body
as beautiful as sculpture can capture
          human form.
I could only guess what was here
          before—
This in the light breeze from the water,
          just off the lagoon.
The water plays lap, lap, against
mangrove roots and clusters of oysters,
and a sky, so jet stream blue, because of
          January.
It's the beginning of the new year,
and I observe that her movements cast
her as a golden goddess in the sun.

And now I sit in the living room where
      the Christmas tree is still up.
She sings in the bath to wash the sand
      away...
I hear eastern music, that I have only
      known through the airwaves,
yet now I am here in presence.

And I sit on the couch, and I wonder
      about this journey,
I feel I've travelled so far...
I wonder and she really has me thinking.
And I felt lucky because I travelled her
      mind in the Gulf coast sun;
she gives me long memories, etched and
      burned into blue glass.

The Drive

Darkness rolls in—
dim lights, city lights.
Leonard Cohen's last breath
shrouds the road in full night.
Dead stare to blinking eyes—
new iterations in October moon.

On Your Honor

I want to face myself.

        It's only me,

                no one else.

I Fal
   l

   o
   f
   f

   t
   h
   e

   e
   d
   g
   e

and wonder if I was wrong—

        DON'T KNOW.

           I wander far in the dark,

lonely to be on my own.

        Split as my he↓art—on your honor.
— —
Sink, not swim,
        like a stone.

Mad Hatter's

Sick to my stomach,
but we still made conversation.
It was dark as we drove
in the headlight glare.

We stopped on the way;
drank exotic teas at Mad Hatter's
in the Queen of Hearts corner;
our hearts on the wall melting.

It was Halloween;
I wanted to make the best of it,
and let it all sink in—
I wanted to let myself be with you,

while you wrote 53
compliments in my notebook,
and poems about light and dark,
and the prince of all darkness.

I thought it curious—
I let myself be with you.
And loved you for all of it
while the hookahs crackled.

And shadowy figures
played cards in corners,
while we sat in our corner;
our shadows still there today.

Dream #4

Late night when the moon is up,
on a road numbered 266.

This is the hear and now.
The tires meet the road—gliding.

Steering wheel with the old familiar
luminescence of moon.

I can see the veins in my hands
as they grip with intense life.

Imagined blood through blue veins,
and the heartbeat's swooshing tempo.

Soft and unspoken in light that's
bouncing off the dashboard.

Ricochet shadows on my jeans—
I can see the veins in my hands.

All alone—digital clock says 12:32 AM;
like a ghost moving fast,

through time and space—moon!
And crossed a bridge into the pale light.

The Sun Still Set on the Horizon

"Beer tastes better in the open air."
Reminds me of so long ago;
long gone away and not so young
          anymore.

"When you were young you'd...
Acting like it was the end of the world,
but the sun still set on the horizon."

There's a calming stillness out here,
and I'm okay...
I'm feeling okay.

Ghost Town

All is calm tonight.
You're on my mind.
It's okay...

Let down.

What was—
ghost town.
Can't force a mood.

The future looms;
give peace
to my heart.

Move on.

My blood.
Your blood.
Our children.

Our love.

I know the truth.
Won't see in you.
I tried.

Hearts change.

Mirror Image

Eyes red with sin—
Looking into the mirror
in the church bathroom.
I see Judas... at very best.

Jesus sat at the well;
listened to the Samaritan woman.
I pray at the bathroom sink
and I hear no answers—no clarity.

Man was not created
to be alone,
yet sometimes it feels
I have walked alone.

Crossroads

We're at a crossroads,
           and we need to know;
to test our baptismal waters.

We're like ghosts coming out of the
           woodwork,
like free spirts floating in evening fields
           after the rain.

Yet, I can make no decision—
I can see that hurts you.

But I am not your phantom love.
I am not the green of early summer
           that you remember.

To look out amongst the trees,
and declare your freedom is bold,

but could never be the tangles of our
youth—our bodies, hearts, and minds.

Summer Spirits

kites float like angels
just above the treetops.

where purple clouds crack
in the heavy summer haze.

like spirits come home
here and gone again.

as spirits returning
like lost generations.

they float like angels
right above the treetops.

Beneath the Oak

When all there is—
the need to be quiet.
An angel's gaze—
an angel's face written in sky.
We sit still and breathe.

We sit quietly, talking.
We talk about nothing—
nothing important.
We laugh at nothing—
nothing worth mentioning.

We let quiet hands calm,
while you decide what it is—
what you are made for.
What you are made to do,
while I decide what is wanting.

And sunlight turns low,
and summer summons green,
and evening's gentle breeze,
and coolness beneath the oak,
while birds pull veil of night.